Angels

Go

Naked

Also by Cornelia Nixon

Now You See It

Angels

Go

Naked

Cornelia

Nixon

COUNTERPOINT

WASHINGTON, D.C.

This book is a work of fiction. Names, characters, places,
and incidents either are products of the author's imagination or are used fictitiously. Any resemblance to actual
events or persons, living or dead, is entirely coincidental.

Library of Congress Cataloging-in-Publication Data

Nixon, Cornelia.
    Angels go naked: a novel in stories / Cornelia Nixon.
        p. c.m.
    ISBN 1–58243–062–4 (alk. paper)
    1. Dual-career families—California—Berkeley—
Fiction. 2. Dual-career families—Illinois—Chicago—
Fiction. 3. Berkeley (Calif.)—Fiction. 4. Marital prob-
lems—Fiction. 5. Married people—Fiction. 6. Chicago
(Ill.)—Fiction. 7. Childlessness—Fiction. I. Title.

PS3564.I94 A84 2000
813'.54—dc21

                                                    99–057278

                        FIRST PRINTING

            Book design by Victoria Kuskowski

                        COUNTERPOINT
                        P.O. Box 65793
                Washington, D.C. 20035-5793

    Counterpoint is a member of the Perseus Books Group.

            10 9 8 7 6 5 4 3 2 1

*For Dean Young, Tony Hoagland,
Lisa Ruddick*

Contents

The Women Come and Go

~~~~~~~~~~~~~

One-quarter of her waking life had gone to practicing the violin, but when her teacher entered her in a national audition, she was surprised to make it to the finals and didn't bother checking the results. The teacher had to track her down at home to tell her she'd won. Margy knew it was a fluke, but within a month she was invited everywhere to play (to Tanglewood, to Aspen, with the Boston Symphony), and at her school in the Back Bay, where she'd always had to practice straight through lunch, ignored by everyone, suddenly she had so much cachet that the most sought-after girls were seeking her. Ann was generally acknowledged to be the most beautiful girl in school, and beautiful in a way that made other girls feel awe: she was perfect in the natural state, like Grace Kelly before she met the prince, only better, since she'd never bleached her hair or worn lipstick. She had a nunlike aura and wore expensive modest clothes, the kind that most girls' mothers picked for them and they refused to wear. Even the Huntington uniform looked good on her. Calluses did not grow on her toes. Whatever she said was considered wise. She liked to quote from Herman Hesse, Kahlil Gibran, and other sources of deathless wisdom.

"Just sit on your bed and think," she said. Hushing to listen, girls went home and sat on their beds.

And with Ann came Elizabeth, her lifelong acolyte. Their mothers were friends, former debutantes who had married the wrong men and now lived in a neighborhood much faded from its former glory instead of in three-story mansions out in Brookline or Lexington. Elizabeth dressed like Ann, even vied with her a little in the neatness of her gestures, the propriety of her shoes. But she didn't have the face, or the hair or the skin, and no one stopped to listen when she talked, unless it was about Ann.

"As Ann said to me last night," she might begin, through a din of girlish voices, and suddenly a hush would fall.

Then in their junior year they took on Margy, who was related to no debutantes, whose hair was impossible, maggot-white and curled as tight as Velcro in tiny fetal snarls, who was always fidgeting and humming and dancing with her bony legs when she wasn't playing violin. But she learned fast, and soon the three of them were gliding modestly around the school, discussing Robert Lowell or Sylvia Plath, looking benignly (but silently) at the other girls. Ann and Elizabeth would listen to Margy practice during lunch, and after school they all walked home with Ann (who lived only a block away, on "hardly passionate Marlborough") or out in every weather to the Esplanade, where they would grieve together privately, for the divorce of Elizabeth's parents, and the death of Margy's mother when she was only twelve, and the last cruel thing Ann's had said to her.

"'Could it be then that this was life?'" Ann quietly intoned one brilliant winter day beside the Charles, the sky delft blue, the river frozen blistering white. "'Was there no safety? No learning by heart of the ways of the world? No guide, no shelter, but all was miracle, and leaping from the pinnacle of a tower into air?'"

In their senior year, they read Camus in French and took on existential responsibility, marching gravely, all in black, with a hundred thousand others up and down the major avenues to protest the bombing of North Vietnam. Margy started quoting from the things she'd read, but without Ann's authority: she might just mutter quietly, so no one else could actually hear, "'Quick eyes gone under earth's lid,'" or *"'Il faut imaginer Sisyphe heureux.'"* On her birthday in November, Elizabeth and Ann gave her a locket with their three initials in a triangle, and for Christmas they all gave each other books, disapproved together of their family celebrations, and went to midnight mass at Holy Cross, for the music, and to appall their parents, none of whom were Catholic or in danger of becoming so. Away from Huntington they were more free, and sometimes, standing on street corners, waiting to cross in the winter sun, Ann and Elizabeth might fall in with Margy's dance, gently snapping fingers, tapping feet. Crazed with success, she once vamped off a curb into the path of a careening cab, but they yanked her back in time.

Margy was happy to be their friend, though she knew she was not like Ann. She had calluses not only on her toes but on every finger of both hands, and had once had a hickey on her neck. She'd gotten it from a pianist named Gary Slade, on whom she'd had a crush until the night he tried to make her fish the car keys from his underpants. She had walked home that night, and never been alone with any guy since then, but still she went on having similar effects on other boys and men. The chorus master at her music school was a handsome man, but he was past her father's age, and if she looked at him it was only on obligatory Saturdays, singing husky alto in the second row. But at the last school picnic out at Marblehead, he'd gotten her off by herself, both of them in bathing suits, not fifty yards from where her father stood. Running a pool cue through his toes, he'd said, "You know I want to make love to you," as if she were accustomed to hearing words like that, when she was just sixteen and had been kissed exactly once, by Gary Slade.

She'd never mentioned these events to Elizabeth and Ann. In fact, she would have died on the rack before she did. But once she told her father about Gary Slade, in vague theoretical terms, as if it were simply something she had heard, to see whose fault he thought it was. Her father was an architect, and he liked theoretical problems, though preferably the geometrical kind. He was willing to talk about anything, however, after dinner, when he'd had a few martinis just before.

"Well, now," he said, running one bony hand across his hair, which sprang up in a solid hedge as his hand passed, curled like Margy's, only slightly red. "That would depend on how she got into the car, now, wouldn't it?" If she had kissed the man and led him on, then it was her fault too. He thought in general women were too quick to speak of rape. Leaning one elbow on the table, he held the other hand out in the air and looked at it.

"When a gal shows up at the precinct and says she's been raped, they make her hold a hand out, and check to see if it's trembling. Because if it is, it means she had an orgasm, and it wasn't rape."

He glanced at Margy, looked away, fair cheeks flushing clear red.

"Of course, sometimes it is." He grinned, as if he knew he shouldn't say what he was going to next. He gave her a bold look. "But when it does happen, when it can't be stopped. Why not just relax, and enjoy?"

In January of their senior year, Ann was elected queen of the winter festival at a boys' school across town, by guys she'd mainly never met, and Margy and Elizabeth went with her as her court, flanking her at the hockey match, triple-dating to the ball that night. Ann chose as her escort Gary Slade, who was still the best-looking young man they knew, while Margy (having no one else to ask) went with his little brother, Jason, with whom she'd shared a violin teacher since they were six.

The night of the ball she rode in Gary's car as if she'd never seen it before. She didn't have to talk to him, or even much to Jason. She was really there with Elizabeth and Ann, as they were there with her. Gary had to stand for hours by the throne the boys had made for Ann, while she sat silent and expressionless, in a white ball gown and rhinestone crown, bearing the stares of all those eyes. When the ball was over, they asked to be delivered back to Ann's, where they dismissed their escorts at the curb (Gary trailing after Ann forlornly, saying, "Can I call you soon?") and went in to drink hot chocolate while Margy pranced in her long skirt from room to room, too excited to sit down.

"Gary should be falling on his sword by now," Elizabeth noted, smiling down into her mug.

Lifting her lovely head, Ann seemed to consider an object far away. "Gary? Oh, Gary will be fine. He'll get married and buy a house and have five children and become 'a sixty-year-old smiling public man.'"

Margy was fidgeting nearby. Suddenly she felt bold.

"'The women come and go,'" she said. "'Talking of Michelangelo.'" And then, with special glee, "'I do not think that they will sing to me.'"

Ann laughed, and kissed her cheek. She put a record on, and they all began to dance, to "Let It Bleed" and "Love in Vain," and "You can't always get what you want, but if you try sometime you just might find you get what you need," until they had calmed down enough to sleep, Elizabeth with Ann in her canopy bed, Margy on a cot down at the foot.

~

Margy started reading through her father's library, leather-bound classics hardly touched by anyone, and after sampling here and there she settled on the Sigmund Freuds, which were small and dense and rewarding even in small bites, and therefore suitable for reading in the moments when she wasn't practicing. She read Dora, Anna O., *Civilization and Its Discontents*. She took to peppering her talk with Freudian remarks.

"I have cathected to those shoes," she'd say. "The economics of my libido may require a chili dog." Or, "Time to get obsessional about that test."

One week she was excused from classes in the afternoons to rehearse with the Boston Symphony, and as she waited for the T at Arlington, she read that if a woman dreams her daughter is run over by a train, that means she wants to go to bed with the man who once gave her flowers as she got onto a train. She was about to turn the page when she felt a hard stare from a few feet off. Pretending to read on, she tapped out the timing of the Paganini she was going to play against one edge of the book, as if deeply engrossed.

The staring did not stop. Annoyed, she glanced that way and recognized the new girl in her class at Huntington. Rachel had arrived only that year, a tall, dark, awkward girl with huge black eyes who stared at everyone as if she found them very strange, and slightly amusing. Imitating Ann's most unrevealing expression, Margy gave her a brief nod and returned to her book, the most effective of the small, polite rejections she and Ann and Elizabeth practiced every day on other girls at school.

Rachel moved closer, staring like a baby over its mother's shoulder. She read the spine on Margy's book. Her voice squeaked in amazement.

"Are you holding that right side up?"

Margy finished the sentence and looked at her. Rachel's uniform was entirely disguised by a black leather jacket and beret, her hair whacked off around the earlobes. But her face was fresh and artless as a two-year-old's.

"Insulting people in train stations is a sign of unresolved dilemmas in the inner life."

Rachel chuckled, watching her. "And what about the virgin goddess, does she read books too?"

Margy pretended not to know who she could mean, narrowing her eyes at her. "Why aren't you in school?"

Rachel whipped out a pass and twirled it in the air.

"Legal as milk," she said, but grinning in a way that made it clear she wasn't going to the dentist after all. She had a sick friend at B.U., and how could she leave her there alone, pining for a cool hand on her brow?

"Freud used to operate on people's noses," Rachel calmly said. "To clear up their sexual hang-ups. He thought if you put your fingers in your purse you were playing with yourself. He was a little bit hung up on cock, and thought the rest of us were too."

Margy rode with her to Copley, slightly stunned. On the platform, changing trains, she glanced back at the one she had just left, and there was Rachel pressed against the glass, eager as a puppy locked inside a car.

She introduced her to Elizabeth and Ann, and soon Rachel started showing up at lunch, refusing to fade off as other girls had learned to do. She even followed on their private walks, stalking behind them with her long, unhurried gait.

"What about me?" she would actually cry, throwing her arms out wide, as they tried to walk away.

She introduced them to new lore, Simone de Beauvoir and *The Story of* O and *The Tibetan Book of the Dead*, and gradually to other things. Rachel had lived in Paris and L.A. and Israel, but now her parents had moved to Beacon Hill, a few blocks from the house where Margy'd always lived, and she took to turning up on Sunday afternoons, to listen to her play and go for walks and tell her things that would have made Margy's mother's hair stand up. Already Rachel had a lot of friends, older women living on their own, who fed her marvelous meals, peyote buds, and grass, and taught her unimaginable acts in bed. She kept her fingernails cut to the quick so that they could not wound. She said she could do anything a man could do, only better, because she was a girl too.

"There's nothing nicer than getting ready for bed," she said, "knowing there's a girl in there waiting for you."

Margy listened, thrilled and shocked. She began to look back with new eyes on certain things she'd done herself. The summer after her mother died, a rash of slumber parties had gone through her neighborhood, with girls she hardly knew at Huntington. But Margy had gone to every one, and when the lights were out they'd played a secret game. Bedded in their sleeping bags on some girl's living room rug, they'd touched each other's breasts, circling incipient nipples with light fingertips, until the hostess said to switch, and then the one you had just touched would do the same to you. They did it as a dare, to prove that they were brave, and they would have all dropped dead to learn that it had anything to do with sex—though the boldest girls, who had invented it, played an advanced form of the game, removing pajama pants and circling fingertips on a certain sensitive spot. Torture, they called that.

"Who were they?" Rachel squeaked, dropping to her knees on the Common, clutching Margy's coat. It was early spring, the air cold and sweet, and they were loitering after a rally against the bombing of Cambodia. "Please, please, pretty please. Tell me. Are they still at Huntington?"

Most of them were, but Margy said they had all moved away. Rachel sank her hands into the pockets of her leather jacket, slouching morosely down the path.

"Why do I never meet girls like that? I just meet little virgin straights. Not that you aren't cute, of course," she said, and tousled Margy's hair.

Margy assumed that Ann knew nothing of Rachel's other life, and that it would be best to keep it to herself. Then one Sunday she called Ann's, and Ann's mother said that she and Rachel had gone out. Another time she stopped by, on her way home from music school, and found Rachel cooking in the kitchen with Ann's mother. Ann's mother was formal and remote and tall, a suntanned woman in yachting clothes who smoked and watched you without smiling while you spoke. Margy was afraid to say a word to her, and she had always called her Mrs. Church. But in the kitchen she was laughing, deep and slow, stabbing a spoon into a pot, while Rachel watched her, hands on hips.

"Betsy! Not like that!" Rachel cried, and tried to wrestle the spoon away from her, both of them laughing like maniacs.

Margy stood chuckling in the kitchen doorway. Mrs. Church whirled at the sound, face sobering at once.

"Oh, hello, Margaret. Annie's in her room, I think."

Margy stood on one foot, smiling, but they did not go on. Dutifully, she went to look for Ann as peals of giggles echoed from the kitchen walls.

~

That spring, Margy fell in love. Yale was taking women now, and her father'd asked her to apply, since he had gone there, and to try it for at least a year instead of Juilliard. To help convince her, he arranged for her to meet the son of a new partner in his firm, who was finishing at Yale and would be entering the law school in the fall. Henry Bergstrom was handsome and sandy-haired like Gary Slade, but soft-spoken and grown-up and kind, with broad shoulders and a narrow waist and one chipped tooth that gave his grin a boyish charm. He was from New York City, had lived in Texas and Brazil, his family having only recently relocated to Boston, and he was a fan of *carnaval* and soccer as well as football and World War II. His voice thrilled her, deep and faintly drawling, but abrupt and furtive when he was moved.

"Where have you been?" he would say quickly on the phone, as if in pain, when she'd been practicing too long. But in person he might hold an ice-cream cone out too high, focus his eyes above her head, and gravely search for her. The Brazilians had a dozen words for "shorty" and "little kid," along with maybe a hundred each for "pester," "scram," and anything to do with sex, though he wouldn't tell her what they were.

"Hey, *pixote*, what's it to you?" he would say when she asked, or call her *tico-tico, catatau.*

He took her to the symphony, where he listened with shining eyes, turning at the end to say he'd rather hear her play. She gave a solo recital in June, and he sat up straight and rapt beside her dad.

"Pretty good for a *pixote*," he whispered in her ear, standing by protectively as Ann and Elizabeth and Rachel all surged up to kiss her cheek. He drove a powder-blue MG, and Rachel called him Ken, after the boyfriend of the Barbie doll.

"Is *Ken* coming up this weekend *again?*" she'd say, staring with outraged onyx eyes.

Margy got into Yale, and agreed to give it a try. Henry came home to Boston for the summer, worked for his dad, and she saw him almost every night. They went to hear the Pops, and to restaurants a few times, then settled into eating with her father or his parents, and after dinner going for a walk. Henry didn't really like to go out at night.

"When I'm married, I won't go anywhere at all," he said, blue eyes warm. "I'll have my own fun at home."

The last thing every night before he left, in the car or on her porch or in her living room, he'd lean close and kiss her a few times, always stopping before she wanted to. Once he pulled her down onto his parents' couch, stopped as if switched off, and apologized. On the way home he talked about the beauty of *carnaval*, how all rules were suspended there ("Don't you ever go to one," he said, grinning hard, gripping her hand). But a few nights later in the car he slid one hand up her side, where he could feel a little of her breast—stinging her so unexpectedly with want that tears spilled from the corners of her eyes.

"I may have to sign up for a nose job soon," she said one sultry afternoon, twirling on a swing in a park near Rachel's house. Ann was at the Vineyard with her family, and Rachel moped on the next swing, rolling a joint in her lap. "That is, if things go on this way."

Pulling down her heavy black sunglasses, Rachel regarded her with some alarm. "You wouldn't. Not with *Ken?*"

Margy tipped her head back toward the ground, viewing the world upside down. "That's who it's done with," she pointed out. "By virgin straights. The Kens of this world."

Rachel pushed her sunglasses back up over her eyes and looked inscrutable.

"Not necessarily," she finally said, and gave one fleeting grin, though she would not explain.

~

In August Henry's parents left for their summer place down on Long Island, and Henry lingered on alone. At first they pretended nothing had changed, eating at Margy's, taking walks. Then one night he made dinner for some friends from Yale, at his parents' house in Brookline, and invited Margy too. The friends were a couple, tall gazellelike blonds who almost looked alike, both living with their parents for the summer, and happy to be out of their sight.

They all drank gin and tonic before Henry's manly fare (steak and potatoes and oversalted salad), and then the gazelles disappeared, into Henry's bedroom, it turned out, with his war books and his model planes. Margy and Henry climbed up to the widow's walk on the third floor, where they could watch the city lights reflected on the river in the summer dusk, Margy in a dress that tied behind the neck and almost nothing else, Henry in a seersucker jacket. She was quivering lightly, not from cold, and when he ran his fingers down the bare skin of her back, she turned and started kissing him.

Startled, he opened his eyes wide and seized her like a tortured man. Moments later they were in his parents' bed, pressing together through their clothes until she lost all sense of being in a room, or even in a body of her own, apart from his. Then he stopped. Fingers in the tight curls at her scalp, he shook her face from side to side.

"*Negativo, pixote,*" he said, and left the room.

Henry left to join his parents in Wading River, and suddenly her life went blank. She called her friends, but already they seemed remote. She hadn't seen them often over the summer, and Elizabeth and Ann had had a fight, though neither would say why. ("It's me," Rachel explained. "Elizabeth is jealous of the time I spend with Ann.") Margy saw Ann a few times, but never alone, no matter what they planned: when

Ann arrived, Rachel would be with her, grinning and relaxed and full of little jokes. They were both staying home, Ann to go to Radcliffe and Rachel to B.U., and Rachel seemed almost to live at Ann's place now. Her clothes were hung on chairs in Ann's room, and once Margy found her lying on the canopy bed, an arm across her eyes.

"Ann needs support right now," Rachel explained when Margy asked her what was going on. Since they'd left Huntington, Ann's mother had started a campaign against Ann, telling her she was spoiled and self-centered, and other cruel, unnecessary remarks.

"Last year, when your friends found you so charming," Betsy had lately said in reference to the winter festival. Ann's eyes were always shining with leashed tears, and Rachel hovered close to her, one hand on her shoulder, staring at anyone who came near.

"Oh, for God's *sake*," Margy said one hot night in Cambridge as they were walking toward a party full of Rachel's friends. "People's mothers *say* things like that. It's just the ordinary coin of mother-daughter economics. You're lucky that you have a mom at all."

Rachel's mouth fell open as if Margy'd fired a gun. Clutching Ann's shoulders, she steered her away. Later she cornered

Margy at the party, in a throng of loud and happy older women. ("Lay off, she's straight," Rachel kept saying as they stopped to stare.)

"You don't know," she said quietly, watching Margy with a light in her black eyes. "You just don't know. *Comprend-tu?*"

Henry wrote to Margy, in a big angular hand on heavy paper, about his father's need to win at golf, and where they'd sailed that day, and how much he thought of her. Once he said remembering how she'd kissed him on the widow's walk that night was driving him insane. But he didn't trust letters, so he'd say no more. Except he hoped that he could see her the moment she got to Yale. In fact he would be waiting in her college yard.

The night before she left, Ann stopped by with Rachel to give her a blank book with a dove-gray linen cover, for a journal while she was away, and Rachel gave her a God's Eye she had made. Ann was wearing Rachel's leather jacket, clutched around her tightly with both hands. She gazed at Margy with beautiful clear eyes.

"You are coming to a place where two roads diverge, and taking the one less traveled by." She touched Margy's hand. "We understand each other, don't we, Margy? No matter what happens."

Margy followed them out to the street and watched them walk away. In the dark, their heads inclined toward each other till their silhouettes converged.

Her father drove her to New Haven, delivered her to his old college, and took her on a campus tour, pointing out the design of each quadrangle. Then he was gone, and Henry was there, in his seersucker jacket, fingers clenched around her arm.

"Can we go now?" he said quietly, hardly moving his lips.

It was Indian summer, hot sun with an autumn drowsiness, and Henry had the top down on the MG. Quickly crossing town, he raced south. The wind was too loud in the car for talk, but Margy knew where they were going now. She had on a simple sheath of rose linen that Ann had helped her pick out, her hair restrained in a ribbon the same shade. But as they crossed the bridge onto Long Island in late sun, the wind teased out the ribbon and her hair burst free, with a ripple of pleasure along the scalp.

〰

He had her back soon after breakfast, though she'd missed the freshman dinner in her college and had failed to sleep in her bed. Calhoun was full of Southerners, from Georgia and Virginia and the Carolinas, and they were all just trooping off in tennis whites, or to try out for some a cappella group, as she made her way upstairs, trembling slightly and trying to look blasé. At the last second, when the pain was most intense, she had tried to pull away. But Henry went on saying, "Just relax," into her ear, and soon she lay still listening to him sleep, with a feeling she didn't recognize, like floating in a warm bath, with an undertow of fear.

In the morning he had quickly pulled a pillow across the bloodstain on the sheet, as if she shouldn't see that, when she had already seen it in the bathroom twice, in the middle of the night and again after the second time, when he woke her at first light, his lean, hairless chest quivering before her eyes like a wall she had to climb. Driving back, he didn't say a word. The law school had already started, and he had to be in class. But he kissed her tenderly by Calhoun gate in the open car, and said he would be there to pick her up on Friday afternoon.

She took long, meditative showers, spent whole days in the practice rooms, and only joined her fellow frosh in class. On Fridays Henry drove her out to Wading River, where the house was always packed now with his friends, who played tackle on the beach and drank all night, and she was alone with him only in the sandy bed. With a football in his arms he was unexpectedly exuberant, and she watched him from a beach chair in the autumn sun, trying to write something profound to Rachel and Ann. They'd sent her two postcards, one from a small hotel in Provincetown. ("All quite legitimate, you understand," Rachel's part had said. "Searching the beach for pebbles you may have sent. Now is the time to buy a kite.") But Margy had nothing to say that she could trust to letters now, so she watched Henry steal the ball, and laugh and cheat and leap across his fallen friends with lean, tan legs, and streak across the sand to score.

The weather changed, dry leaves crackling in the wind at night. The first cold week, she did not hear from Henry, and on Saturday she called his rooms, where his suitemate said he had gone home to Boston. Margy was concerned. Of course she knew that men could change, from the days of Gary Slade. But the last time she had seen Henry, he had been more tender than before, and had held her hand on the long drive back to Yale.

Monday night, on her way home from the practice rooms, she stopped by the law school dorm, where he was studying. He seemed surprised but glad, and pulled her in protectively.

"Everything all right?" he said, ushering her quickly into his room, shutting the door. "Nothing wrong?"

They talked politely, sitting on the bed, his law books lit up on the desk. He did not explain why he'd gone home to Boston, and she didn't ask. When she rose to go, he said goodbye at the door and watched her leave. He strode behind her down the gleaming brown expanse of hall.

"Don't go," he said, clutching her arm and looking at the floor. "Please stay, all right?"

She couldn't sleep in his narrow bed, and she got up late to walk back through the cold, clear night. That weekend she practiced all the daylight hours, avoiding telephones. But when she went back to Calhoun at night, there were no messages for her. She called Henry's rooms, pretending to have a French accent.

"Boston," his suitemate said.

"Ah, *bon*," she said, and did not call again.

~

Henry wrote her a careful letter, saying he had made a mistake and wasn't ready to be serious yet, but asking her to let him know if she ever needed anything from him. Margy wrote four versions of a letter back, outraged, pleading, miserable, abject, and tore them up. Finally she sent a postcard with a view of Wading River (bought to send to Rachel and

Ann), saying she was always glad to hear from him but didn't think she would be needing anything. He sent her a biography of Freud, which she had already read ("From your friend, Henry," it said inside), and a yard of rose-colored ribbon to replace the one she'd lost while riding in his car. Once she saw him on Elm Street, idling in traffic as the snow fell on the cloth top of his car. Honking and waving, he half emerged. But she saluted with her violin and hurried off against the traffic, so he couldn't follow her.

Sleet was rattling on the windows as if hurled from fists on the day she started to throw up. She tried to make it stop, lying on her bed in the hot blasts from the heating ducts, as Rachel's God's Eye twirled above. It was ridiculous, it was impossible. Henry had been so cautious, breaking open little hard blue plastic cases, exactly like the ones she'd seen once in her father's dresser drawer when her mother was alive, and dropping them beneath the bed as he put their contents on. The night she'd visited his room, she had crouched to count the empties in the silvery light, and there had been at least a dozen more than he had used that night. Though it was hard to tell, of course, how old they were.

She went to class and could not hear a word. She could not play the violin, or remember why she'd ever wanted to.

The nausea surrounded her, six inches of rancid blubber through which she had to breathe. She threw up in the daytime, in the evening, in the middle of the night. She told herself to just relax. Morning sickness is all in the woman's head, Freud said. She ate a crust of hard French bread, and saw it unchanged moments after in the white cup of the toilet bowl.

She found a doctor down in Bridgeport, where she would not run into anyone from Yale. The man she picked had chosen his profession because the forceps used at his own birth had damaged a nerve in his face, causing his forehead to hang down across his eyes, while his mouth pulled to one side. Yes, he had good news for her, he said. Mrs. Henry Bergstrom, she had called herself, and lied about her age. Alone with him when the nurse had left, she mentioned that they weren't quite married yet. The doctor may have given her a kindly look, though it was hard to tell.

"Don't be upset if something happens to it," he said, lips flapping loose around the sounds. "It's not because it's out of wedlock or anything like that. It's not your fault."

Margy nodded, and started to weep quietly. Moments later she was on the sidewalk in cold sun, with the recommended diet in her purse, and Mrs. Henry Bergstrom's next appointment card.

She'd be a famous violinist, live in a garret with the child. It would be a purse-sized child, round and pink, a girl, never growing any bigger or needing anything, and it would ride on Margy's chest while she played the major concert stages of the world. She would wear flowered dresses, cut severely (bought in France), with black berets and leather jackets. She would smoke fat cigarettes through vermilion lips, drink liqueur from a small glass. And one day, in a café on the Boul' Mich', or in Nice, or in her dressing room in Rome, Henry would track her down. He'd send his card backstage, and she would send it back. She'd look the other way in the café.

"Mais non, monsieur," she'd say. "We do not know each other. *Excusez moi."*

For Thanksgiving she had to fly to Florida with her father and pretend to eat some of the thirty pounds of turkey her grandmother made, and throw up in the bathroom of the tiny oceanview apartment with the fan on and the water running. Back at Yale, she learned that she had failed midterm exams (equipped with the vast wasteland of all she hadn't read), and packed to leave for Christmas break.

Rachel met her train. Sauntering down the platform, thumbs hooked into black jeans, she looked very young in a new black motorcycle jacket with silver chains. But her stare was just the same.

"They're engaged," she said, with a tragic face.

Margy kissed her on both cheeks, said, what? and who? and even laughed. She felt a little better, having not thrown up almost all day.

Rachel hung suspended, watching her. Slowly a look of wonder, almost delight, broke on her face. Stepping closer, she took tender hold of Margy's head.

"Oh, baby. Don't you know anything yet?"

~~

It had started in the summer, Rachel said, when she and Ann first went to bed. They'd been in love since spring—she and Ann, that is—and Rachel was spending all her time at Ann's by then. Ann never wanted her to leave, but at first they didn't get near the bed. They'd sit on the floor in her room and talk until they fell asleep, right where they were. Ann couldn't face it, what it meant, or do more than kiss Rachel on the cheek.

"She was just a little virgin straight," Rachel explained. "Like you, only worse. She thought that girls who went to bed with girls would end up riding Harley-Davidsons and stomping around in big dyke boots. It wasn't possible for the queen of the winter festival."

Then suddenly it was, and they'd been lovers now for months, every night in the canopy bed. It was the most intense thing in her life, and in Ann's. One night they'd been making love for hours when she touched Ann's back, and it was wet.

"That does it," Rachel'd told her then. "No matter what, you can't go saying you're a virgin now."

Things were good then for a while. They took some little trips. ("You lied to me on that postcard," Margy pointed out, and Rachel shook her head. "I promised her," she said.) Ann was jealous of Rachel's other friends, and accused Rachel of not loving her—while she, Ann, was in love for life. But Rachel reassured her, and then things were all right. Even Betsy laid off Ann.

"Betsy thinks I'm good for her," Rachel said, and grinned. "She likes the way Ann shares her toys with me." Of course Betsy had no idea what was going on, it wasn't in her lexicon. But she liked Rachel, they got along. And Rachel learned to head Betsy off when she was going after Ann.

Then one night in the fall, Ann announced that she was going out, and Henry showed up at the door. He took her out to eat, and to a play, and to the symphony.

"They went *out?*" Margy cried, but Rachel only looked at her. Out, and home to meet his parents too. It was a bulldozer through their happy life. He started calling every night from Yale. Ann would take the call in her parents' room and close the door. She started quoting Henry. He said men should always be gentle to all women, and he was sorry it had not worked out with Margy, but that they had parted friends. This was the time in their lives that counted most, he said, when the steps they took would determine all the rest, and it was important to be circumspect. Ann agreed, and every weekend circumspectly she went out with Henry, and came home to sleep with Rachel.

"So now she's wearing this big Texas diamond that used to belong to his grandmother. And all she does is cry. He brings her home, and she gets in bed with me and starts to cry. She cries while we make love, and then cries in her sleep. In the morning she gets up to try on her trousseau, and puts on sunglasses so Betsy won't see, but they just dam up the tears, until she's got this pool behind them on her cheeks. She's just afraid, and she knows it, but that doesn't mean a thing. They've got the guest list all made out. She's going to marry him in June."

~

Margy took the T to Cambridge, looked for Rachel's friends. She found the one who'd had the party, a big-breasted woman in a T-shirt with short rough hair, who offered to make tea, or lunch, or roll a joint. Yes, she could tell Margy where to go, and no, she wouldn't mention it to Rachel if she didn't want her to. But was she sure?

"It's not a nice thing to go through," she said as she followed Margy out onto the landing, carrying a large gray cat. "Don't do it by yourself, baby."

Margy thanked her, put the number in her purse, but did not make the call. First, she needed to understand. She needed to see Ann one more time, from a distance, preferably. Maybe that would be safe. Maybe then the thing that happened when you looked at her would not, and she would understand, why all their lives arranged themselves Ann's way, as if they were the notes and she was the melody.

Christmas Eve, Margy played chess with her father, which he had taught her as a child, but she was too sick to concentrate, and he won both games. Humming happily, he went off to bed, and she sat waiting in the ornate living room, still decorated in her mother's taste, Persian rugs and heavy velvet drapes and lamps held up by enslaved caryatids ("early sadomasochist," as Rachel'd labeled it). When she could hear nothing but the antique clocks, ticking out of sync, she eased her coat out of the closet, and the bolt out of the door.

Flagging a cab was easier than she'd supposed, with the neighbors all returning home, and she was early for the service at Holy Cross. The cathedral was already nearly full, rows churning with genuflection, kneeling, crossing, touching lips, and she took up a position to one side, beneath a statue of the Virgin, plaster fingers open downward as if beckoning the crowd to climb up into her arms. In an organ loft somewhere above, someone was playing Bach's most schmaltzy fugue, hamming it up with big vibrato on the bass, while in the aisles people streamed both ways, like refugees from war, out toward the doors and in for midnight mass. Their coats were black and brown and muddy green, with sober scarves and hats, and when Ann's head emerged from beneath the outer arch, hair glowing like ripe wheat and freshly cut to brush the shoulders of her camel-hair coat, she seemed to light the air around for several feet.

Margy pressed back closer to the wall. She hadn't forgotten how beautiful Ann was, but memory could never quite live up to her. Henry's shoulders framed her head, wide and straight in a navy overcoat, with Rachel tall as he was next to him, looking strangely wrong in a lace collar, wool coat, and heels. None of them had time to glance across the nave. Rachel was clowning for Henry, rolling her eyes and gesturing with her hands, and he gave a grim smile, looking handsome but harassed, as he stepped up to take Ann's hand. Rachel moved to her other side, and together they maneuvered to a spot behind the final row of pews.

Now all three stood, Rachel and Henry crowded close on either side of Ann, bantering above her head, while she looked docile as a child, and lost. Henry had a firm grip on her hand, and he kept it well displayed, curled against his chest or resting on the pew in front or in his other fist. Ann's other hand was out of sight, but Rachel's arm pressed close to hers, and both their hands plunged down behind the pew, as still as if they'd turned to stone.

Ann leaned back her head, looking high up toward the ceiling, a parted sea of water shining in her eyes. She said something to distract the other two, and all three of them looked up, as if they could see something descending from above. In a moment, other people near them looked up too.

The Bach swelled to an end, and the crowd pressed in, packing all the spaces on the floor. Forging a path back through stiff overcoats, miasmas of perfume, Margy stepped out into the cold, pure night. She'd seen enough, and as she hurried up the avenue, alive with pinpoint lights, Salvation Army bells, and taxis rushing through the slush, the city opened up around her, smaller than before, while she felt strangely huge, as if she were parading through the air like the Macy's Mickey Mouse balloon. A thousand windows lit up small and bright, no bigger than the hollows in a honeycomb, and for a moment she could almost see inside, into the thousand tiny rooms, where figures crossed, and smiled, hiding their hurts, and wanting the wrong things, and spending long nights in their beds alone.

A Solo Performance

~~~~~~~~~~

Joshua, his name was today, though sometimes it was Jennifer. Leaving her narrow room, going down the dormitory stairs, she could feel him on her chest, warm and heavy, smelling of milk and pee. He'd have a squarish head, pink skin, fair hair wisping up above the baby sling. She could see him as she passed the dining hall, though no one in there could. It was a daydream, postcard from a life she didn't have. Stepping out into the warm fall day, leaving her college, crossing the quad, she was just a skinny girl in bell-bottoms, violin pack on her back, with no baby. Yellow maples glowed. Gargoyles grimaced under bright blue sky. A light breeze ruffled ivy on the library. (The baby would enjoy it, and she stopped to show him, in the sun.)

Reaching Elm Street, she checked both ways for picket lines. Once she'd turned the corner, met a barricade of broken chairs, a line of cops in glinting riot shields. But this morning no one seemed to want to stop the war. Only the overachievers were out, heads down on their way to physics, music, math. Head down, she crossed the street (cautious, with the baby on her chest, one hand around his warm, diapered behind).

Across another quad, she could see violinists now, converging from all sides. Lifting her head, she began to walk quickly (steadying the baby with both hands). Now she was Margaret Rose, Violin, who had been picked to do the big Mozart concerto solo with Yale Orchestra. Across the grass, when they saw her, the other violinists slowed, let her beat them to the music school. Striding in, she took the dim steps (careful not to jar the baby) to the floor where Andre's master class would be.

The room was packed already with a crowd of violinists, fidgeting and chewing gum. Here at Yale, she spent a lot of time in rooms completely filled with other string players, and all of them would twitch, check wallets, zippers, the exact location of their instruments, as if obsessive compulsion were an advantage on the violin. Margy took her violin out, tuned, tightened her bow, then loosened it, reclipped her barrettes, adjusted her headband. Straight hair was the only kind in style, but hers curled like some low-grade packing substance, swarm of locusts in her field of vision as she played. Clamping it down, she tuned again, rechecked her bow.

Arching the bow across the strings, she slid into a few bars of the solo, experimentally. Suddenly she felt her belly swell up like a gourd, baby inside, head like concrete, pressed down, stretching her tender parts. Lifting the bow, she let her head tip back. One-two-three, she counted through a big contraction, breathing with the pain. It was just a daydream too, not quite as voluntary as the rest, something her mind would show to her. Eight-nine-ten, she exhaled with the agony.

"Miss Perfect," a voice sneered in a whisper behind her.

Margy sat up. Her belly didn't vanish, but it moved away, became less real. Engaging the bow, she launched into the hardest passage of her solo, tortuous quick changes, lightning triple-stops. She'd practiced it a million times. Her fingers knew it, hands and arms. To show she could, she went on playing for a few beats after Andre strode into the room.

Andre was a big man with an anxious face, dark nervous curls just going gray. When he stood in front of them, all motion stopped. Famous for playing cautiously, he was also famous for harsh praise, and sometimes shattered students casually.

"You are a musical illiterate," he'd said the week before to a young man, in front of the whole class.

Now the room went silent as the inside of a rock. His voice was just above a whisper, but it rose to the ceiling like a cathedral oration.

"The solo in a Mozart concerto is never good enough. The music is always far above your head. Mozart was a genius. You are not."

He swept his hand toward Margy, offering the chance to be never good enough. She raised the bow. Her stomach dropped. Everything she knew about Mozart abandoned her. She wavered through the first few bars.

Andre began to bite his thumbnail, shifted it around to bite the other way. He darted one big hand out in the air. She stopped.

"Hear that? Play that phrase again. You're schmaltzing it. That's junk."

She tried again. He leaped to his feet, made little jagged gestures, pinkie cocked as if above a porcelain teacup.

"Just play the notes, the way they're written! Not like that!"

His black wool legs stood right in front of her. His voice lashed over her. She smelled her sweat. The last allegro seemed a continent away. Why bother, when he wouldn't like it anyway? Tipping her head back, she let her body stretch around the baby's head, pain a high note with vibrato, well sustained. She could no longer hear Andre. Breathing with the big contractions, she closed her eyes and played.

~

At last he strode out of the room. Limp, shirt wet to the waist, she slumped to her knees, slid the violin into its case. All around, the class filed out.

A small Asian woman stopped beside her, standing like a truck driver, one hip jutted to the side, cracking her gum. She was a year ahead of Margy, but she looked about fourteen, straight black hair in ponytails that swung as she moved. She chewed vigorously.

"So, are you nervous when you play, or what? I mean, you know, on stage?"

Margy stood up.

"Nervous? No," she said automatically and stopped. Of course she was, not as bad as when she was a kid. Then she used to throw up, wet the bed. But it seemed bad luck to talk about it, with a solo in three weeks. Better to deny it, like a magic charm.

"When I was a kid, my mother told me just to say, 'These people are in for a real treat,' and sweep out there onto the stage." It had never worked, but it seemed like the right thing to say.

The other violinist did not smile. "'These people are in for a real treat'? Hunh." She left the room.

～

Next afternoon, when Margy showed up at the practice rooms, a trumpeter she knew leaned on a windowsill beside the room she liked to use, eating a sandwich. J.J. had long hair of several kinds, straight blond on top but curly brown below, like pubic hair, with muttonchop sideburns that made him look like a Saint Bernard. She liked J.J., but it was another warm day, peaceful, and she had crossed campus with the baby on her chest. The moment she stepped into the music school, her belly swelled up and the pain bore down on her, too hard to breathe. She breezed by J.J., almost afraid that he might see.

He lifted his sandwich in salute. "Hey. I hear you don't get stage fright."

"Ask me in two weeks."

"Why? You're not going to be scared then either, are you? That's not what I heard."

She paused a beat. So they were out there quoting her. She couldn't think about that now. She had a private lesson in an hour with Andre.

"Don't believe everything you hear, J.J.," she called and closed the door.

~

A week later, the weather changed. Icy clouds swept over New Haven, and one morning the heat came on in her room. In bed, she felt a hot blast from the duct above, and a wave of nausea rolled up her throat. She leaped to her feet, amazed. Daydreams were one thing. Throwing cold water on her face, she rushed out into the frigid air, walked to the music school. But as she stepped into the hot building, her stomach rolled.

She had to practice by an open window in her coat, fingers stiff with cold. Back in her room, she taped the heat duct closed, slept in mittens and a hat. But the next day was the same: in the heated dining room, she looked at foods she had thrown up the year before, and had to leave. She couldn't sit in class. Blue veins started rising underneath her skin, delicate green circles at the eyes. She hadn't slept with anyone but Henry, ever, and she hadn't seen him for a year. Meeting her own eyes in the mirror, she tried to communicate with buried portions of her brain.

"So, do you really think you're still pregnant? Or is it just nostalgia for that happy time?"

She thought of going back to see the doctor with the hanging face. But what could she tell him this time? That she had daydreamed just a little bit too much, and now her mind was going to make her live through it again? Surely it would stop. She went back to the Mozart, windows open to the cold.

～

Rehearsals started, in a heated room. She got herself well chilled, lying on a frozen marble slab, and dove into the stifling interior. Her chair stood in the inner circle of the orchestra, rows of bodies radiating heat. Her stomach heaved, seasick on its rolling inner tide. The conductor was a famous white-haired visitor up from New York, and his cheeks produced two furious red patches at even a small mistake by any member of the orchestra. Fifty string players watched

Margy, waiting for the moment when the error would be hers.

She tried to banish daydreams of all kinds. But as she crossed campus, an eighteen-wheeler truck roared through the light on Elm, and instantly she saw herself beneath it, bones crushed, breasts sheared off. Gasping, she stood, face in hands. In the practice room, windows open to the cold, she turned her head and saw a rifle poked in through one, aimed at her. But when she whirled to look, the air outside was empty, innocent, two floors off the ground.

Two days before the concert, she passed a woman on the curb outside the music school who smiled and handed her a flyer with a brightly colored photograph.

"PAY ATTENTION," it said. "SOMEONE WANTS TO MAKE THIS LEGAL IN YOUR COUNTRY."

The photo underneath was expensively produced, red and white and blue, tiny hands and feet, small curved spines and bulging eyes, tender see-through skin. A bucketful, in fact, ripped in half, sauced with blood.

Margy made it just inside the first-floor women's room and threw up in a sink. Quickly she washed her face. This wasn't happening. She had a concert, she was fine. Shredding the photograph, she flushed it down three toilets, a few flakes at a time.

J.J. was outside his practice room, closing cardboard in the doorjamb, stuffing a towel underneath, so no one could hear him practicing. He hadn't hung around her room lately, but she rushed up to him, glad to see a friendly face.

"J.J.," she cried. "I just threw up."

He toed the towel into place.

"You, Itzhak? That can't be true. And here we are, all waiting for our treat."

She giggled nervously, then noticed his face. He watched her, not smiling. She stepped back a pace.

"Jesus, J.J."

He finished with the towel, smiled to himself. He stood up straight.

"Remember what they say, baby. It's lonely at the top."

Pinching her cheeks between his thumb and fingers, he gave her face a little shake.

"Lo-oo-onely," he said and stepped inside the door.

~

The stage was hot. Dry air whirled up from the floorboards like a wind from hell. Beyond the bright lights shining in her eyes, the audience roared quietly, finding seats, rustling programs. Her father had driven down from Boston, but she could not see him. She could see bored men in black suits, strange women in furs, sneering music students slouched in cheap seats, high up underneath the balconies. Since the nausea's return, her nose had been acute, and a smell rolled toward her now, perfume, mothballs, sour after-dinner breath. Blue cheese, garlic sausage, gin.

She tuned the violin, though she had done it twice already in the warm-up room. Lifting the bow, she felt a rill of nausea begin. Stopping, she concentrated on the cool black velvet skirt that slid across her legs. She had worn nothing underneath, and she saw a flash of a cool beach, Wading River, open sea. Henry had married Ann in June, and she had moved down here with him. They might have seen her name for this concert. She peered out past the lights. Her stomach lurched. She felt a sudden need to stand up, take her violin, and walk offstage.

Too late. To a scatter of applause like rain, the concert master was parading in, Andre's favorite student, a tall, precise young man with two curls drooped over his forehead. The chair beside hers groaned, and the caustic florals of his deodorant swept over her. The conductor swept in like a man who had no time to give this puny orchestra, and she sat up, caught the stagelights in her eyes, played through the opening Beethoven with the other violins.

The Beethoven was over much too soon, and the conductor dashed out, not pausing to bow. The concert master turned and looked down at her, thin lips firm, violin held lightly on his knee. "Don't drag the allegro this time. And try not to smile so much. Do you realize you always smile when you play? It's a little disconcerting for the rest of us. You must realize, it looks a little smug."

Margy's lips parted. She couldn't organize her tongue. *Smile?* She *smiled?*

He turned back toward the audience, which had started to applaud again, as the conductor almost goose-stepped from the wings. He popped up on the stand, nailed Margy with his eyes, flourished both hands.

With a crash of sound, the other instruments came in on the introduction to her first solo. The music galloped past her, huge and fast. She tried to count. Had she lost track? She heard the phrase before the entrance to her solo, lifted her bow, and realized in time, it was the false entrance. Thank heavens she had not started to play. But now adrenaline sloshed through her veins. Her stomach rolled into a long, slow curl. Dizzily she gripped the violin, waited for the nausea to stop, and heard a silence on the stage.

The conductor's finger quivered in the air above her head. The orchestra pulled in its breath, a hundred mouths in one sharp suck. The moment for her entrance had arrived, and passed.

She raised the bow, too slowly. It was a dream. The orchestra was a *Tyrannosaurus rex* with jaws spread wide, waiting for her to step inside. She couldn't move. The concert master turned, stared down at her, eyes frozen wide.

Somehow her fingertips pressed on the strings, her arms moved the bow. Dimly she heard the sounds out of the violin, tone as tinny as a fourth grader on a cigar box tied with string. It was the worst concerto solo ever turned in with Yale Orchestra, and she knew it every second that she played. Eyes fastened on the violin, she made herself keep going, going, to the awful end.

Finally it was over. The audience began to make its roaring sound, like a building falling down. The conductor turned, held out his hand toward her, and even smiled. But she did not rise, and as he strode stage right for the last time, she

stood and plunged straight off into the wings, violinists parting on all sides, as if suddenly recalling things they had to do
offstage.

～

"How do you make a violin concerto a little longer than it
used to be?" it said in green ink, on the wall of her favorite
practice room.

"How do you get a job with the Boston Symphony?" said
purple ink right next to it.

"On your back," said several different hands.

"On your knees."

Next to the words, someone had drawn a life-sized por-
trait of a man in a tuxedo, possibly the new conductor of the
BSO, or maybe Arthur Fiedler, with a curly blond head where
his lap should be. Pointing to it with an arrow was a sign: "Boy,
he's in for a real treat!"

She went back to her room and drew the blinds. She
imagined herself climbing to the roof of the gym, nine stories
up with a rose window near the top, and jumping off. She pictured needles sliding into her veins, injecting her with something that would put her mind to sleep. Taking the only drug
she had, a tranquilizer saved up since her mother's death, she

slept, and dreamed she was on trial, dancing in the courtroom with Ann, while judge and jury watched.

"She did it," Ann said, then swung her arm back and whacked Margy in the face. She woke up, stiff with cold and sick, all the windows open, three A.M.

~

She called the doctor with the hanging face, rode the train down on a gray December day. His waiting room was peaceful, three big-bellied women talking quietly beside a broadleaf plant. Their eyes slid to her stomach as she came in, and she smiled shyly, sank into a chair. With a rush of guilty pleasure, she let the daydream start again. Joshua was home, a teenaged sitter taking care of him, and she was Mrs. Henry Bergstrom, only lately made a mother and already in again, perhaps a wee bit pregnant, ready to be teased. . . .

"Don't you two do anything else for fun?" the doctor might say, wagging one thick finger as he smiled. She would giggle, cheeks flushed, not really ashamed. . . .

A nurse shoved back the cloudy window in the wall, fixed her eyes on Margy. "How are you? Any bleeding, nausea?"

Margy stared at her, lips parted, the flush of pleasure still warm on her cheeks.

The nurse's eyes flicked over her. "What are you now, about nine weeks?"

Margy swallowed, throat so dry it seemed to disappear. The three big-bellied women watched her, smiled. She stood up instinctively.

"That was last year," she barely breathed.

The nurse's head came forward, as if she couldn't hear. She was a tall woman with dyed black hair up in a bun, a big bosom, and glasses on a string. Jamming the glasses on her nose, she studied Margy's chart and threw the glasses off impatiently.

"Where have you been till now?"

The room grew clear and sharp, the beveled glass, the dark green rubber plant, the woman's small but penetrating eyes.

"What happened to your pregnancy?"

～

The car was a Chevrolet Impala, turquoise, with rust, and the man inside had his face hidden in a big black beard, sunglasses, a hat pulled down over the eyes. She had waited for him on a quiet corner of the Back Bay, in a good wool suit, dress flats, a winter coat and brown felt hat, the savings bond her grandmother had given her now rendered down to small bills stuffed into an envelope she held in one gloved hand.

The man slid the money into his coat and handed her a blindfold, soft black cotton like the curtains used for showing films in school. He told her to put it on and lie down in back, using a phony drawl filled with rounded vowels and crisp consonants, an Englishman's attempt to sound American. She lay on the squeaking plastic seat, and he must have driven for an hour, listening to Brahms. The Brahms was followed by an ad for a brokerage firm, read in the deep, tasteful voice of the classical announcer. Then baroque flute music, and the first movement of a Mahler symphony.

Finally they stopped, tires crunching gravel. The back door opened with a groan, and a big hand gripped her arm, Margy staggering passive as a sheep from an hour of being blind. Even through the cloth she could sense the brightening of the air, as if they were near water, hints of diesel oil and rotten crab beneath the snow.

They went through metal-sounding doors into a space that echoed like a warehouse, and on into a smaller room, where sound closed down to nothing when the door was shut. The man backed her to a chair, told her to sit and not to move until she heard him leave the room. Then she was to take the blindfold off, undress, put on the gown that she would find in front of her.

The room was fitted like a doctor's office, skylight above, and very cold. She put on the hospital gown, then her coat. Shivering, she stood barefoot on the cement slab. The sweat was cold beneath her arms, and it smelled sharp as acid, capable of etching steel.

The man came back. His beard was gone, but a surgical mask and cap and gown had him all covered but the eyes, which were blue and watery, with sandy brows.

"On the table," he said, plainly British now. "No coat."

The table was dark green artificial leather, padded underneath, but it felt hard enough to bruise. Gingerly she slid onto it, trying to keep the thin gown closed. The man took hold of her around the hips and hauled them to the table edge. Plugging her bare heels into the stirrups, he propped her knees up toward the sky and spread them wide.

He swabbed her hip and jabbed a needle in. "That's Demerol. It won't help much, but it's all we've got."

She stared up through the skylight, watched a gull cruise by against gray clouds. His hands moved too fast, and at their first touch she leaped, gasping, lips stiff with cold.

"None of that," he said, working something up inside her. "Relax, or you'll be hurt."

The pain inflated out around her, to the ceiling, to the walls, like an explosion in slow motion. She clutched the table, face twisted to one side, drooling on the hard leather. He had not sheeted her, and she could see his bloody fingers and the long-stemmed knives, which he worked inside her, briskly, as if cleaning out a pipe.

"Stop," she gasped out once or twice. No other sounds were in the room, except the rasping of her breath and the mushy clicking of the knives.

Finally he stood up, blood sprayed on his sleeves and freckled on his front. As he moved away from her, the pain diminished, scattering.

He washed his hands. He told her to get dressed and put the blindfold on. She heaved herself upright, delirious.

"Where is it?" She didn't even know what sex it was, or what it looked like, and he did. "Let me see it."

He paused, one hand on the door. His pale eyebrows drifted up, and she could see his lips tug underneath the mask.

"See it? No. You can't see it."

He opened the door.

"It's in little pieces," he added as an afterthought.

～～

She was crying on the table as the doctor with the hanging face put his hands in her. He made it quick, and patted her bare foot.

"You look fine," he said and pulled the sheet down to her feet. "Whoever he was, he did good work."

He stood beside the table, one big hand on her sheeted knee. The wattle of his forehead jiggled slightly.

"Lots of people have disappearing pregnancies."

He glanced at the nurse, who quickly turned and aimed her bun at them. Gathering her clipboard, she left the room. The doctor rubbed his forehead, sighed. He wrote a prescription for tranquilizers.

"Try to relax, you'll get through this. It's just that it goes against your instincts." He squared his shoulders, looked restored to confidence and calm. "The purpose of a woman is to have a child."

Margy sat up. The purpose of a woman? Like the purpose of a spoon? With a flourish, the doctor signed his name, held the prescription out to her.

"Get married, have a nice baby. You'll forget all this."

"Thank you," she managed to say before he left the room. And she did feel grateful, suddenly. It wasn't every day that someone told you what your purpose was, while forgiving you for having failed. He wanted her to know that though she had done something dangerous, illegal, even murderous, it was all right with him. She could still have a nice baby, become one of the nice big-bellied ladies in his waiting room. She tried to picture it, but nothing came in view.

What she could see was this: in a minute, she would walk out to the waiting room, where they'd watch her, knowing what she'd done. And she'd look back, how? A girl with no regrets, relaxed, forgiven, maybe even innocent? It was not a hard performance. She thought she had seen much worse. Sliding off the table, she began to dress for it.

Season of Sensuality

~~~~~~~~~~

The chapel was packed with tasteless Tintorettos, saints with heads cut off, naked sinners plummeting to hell while cheerful cherubs hovered. Wearily Margy and Calvin left and climbed back in the gondola, where Calvin abandoned all pretense, lounging backward so he could stare up at the strong thighs of the gondolier. Calvin was fine-limbed as a Donatello shepherd, in a vanilla suit, white sneakers with no socks, blond stubble like a halo on his head, and he glowed slightly in the fading light. He had been Margy's friend since shortly after college, when they'd spent two nervous years at a London music institute, practicing obsessively (Calvin on the double bass). Now, by some miracle, they had both joined the Chicago Symphony and lived in the same building in Lincoln Park, sharing free time, opinions, sometimes clothes. They'd planned this trip in a therapeutic spirit, both of them in love with the wrong men.

"Not love," Calvin insisted, sighing, as he watched the gondolier. "Pure craven lust. The highest emotion made by God. And that certain je ne sais quoi of knowing they will rip our hearts out in no time."

He had been in love before they left with a trumpeter back home. But so far on this trip, he'd fallen for the steward on their plane, a gang of stevedores in Rome, and the Michelangelo *David*: first the copy in the square, then the real one at the end of the long hallway lined with Slaves.

"How can you stand it, God?" he'd cried, falling to his knees, figures bound in stone around him struggling to get out. "Bring him to life!"

He sighed and stared at the gondolier. "But what would you know about lust?"

Margy sat poised in the center of the seat, where water could not splash on her. The tide cleaned the canals, supposedly, but it was August and you couldn't tell it from the smell. She didn't like to think about the tides, creeping underneath the city streets, ten million tons of marble, ten thousand priceless works of art, and nothing holding them except some ancient wooden posts. Fourteen years before, a flood had nearly washed it all away, and every year the ocean rose a little higher up the walls. From its tower half a mile away, a bell so big it had a name began to swing its massive gong, and the city trembled with the sound as the last glow faded from the air.

The gondola bobbed up to their hotel, and Calvin over-tipped the man as usual, while Margy made her way inside and up the stairs. Tonight she thought she might just have a bath, and go to bed early and read. But Calvin followed her upstairs into her room and threw her closet open, studying her clothes.

"What you need, to wear with all these floral skirts, is a black leather motorcycle jacket with zippers on the sleeves. I saw just the place to look for it today. I'll get Francesco to take us there first thing tomorrow."

"Francesco? So now you know his name?"

He pulled out a thin black dress and held it to his chest. "And maybe something with sequins. A wee bit vampy, maybe, don't you think?"

She went into the bathroom and turned on the brass tap— the pipes moaned. Pulling barrettes out of her hair, she un-dressed and slipped on her kimono.

"See you later," she called. "I'll just have a bath."

He didn't answer, and she stuck her head around the door to make sure he had gone back to his room.

He hadn't left. In fact, he was in her bed, naked and languid. Leaning on an elbow, sheet draped across one slender hip, he pretended to read her copy of *Oggi*.

"Calvin," she said, "you're gay. Your bed's in the other room."

He smiled, patted the sheets. "And these are the last days of empire, a lovely time to be alive. Everyone sleeps with everyone now, remember, dear? Half those creeps in the symphony already assume we do it *every night*, probably *with* the great Michael Sein. Not that I would mind!"

She clutched the kimono closer to her chest. "Really, Calvin, I'm touched, but no. Please get out of here."

Retreating back inside the bath, she bruised her thigh on the bidet. Behind her, his voice rose in a whine.

"Oh, go ahead and save yourself for him. Be a crypto-virgin your whole life. He's *never* going to sleep with you!"

~~

"Don't wear high heels," Andre had said as she prepared for her audition with the Chicago Symphony. She would play behind a screen, but the jury would hear her walking in, and it wasn't wise to let them know she was a woman.

"Jackboots," Andre said. "Big steps, like a man."

Margy considered this advice, then bought a pair of three-inch heels, white linen, open-toed. She was who she was, five feet tall, ninety pounds, female. She also played a piece Andre did not approve, Ravel's "Tzigane." Sinuous and Spanish, littered with acrobatic chords, it was considered not entirely playable, even by Ravel, and Andre advised Mozart instead. The hundred other violinists auditioning agreed, and in the warm-up room half of them were running through the Sonata in E Minor, K.304. But Margy took a chance on the "Tzigane," made the final round, and when the last auditioner had left the stage, stomping in jackboots, she had become the smallest member of a world-class orchestra, though she would sink out of sight when she drew an outside chair, only her hair visible from the good seats on the floor.

The CSO was like a huge, precise machine, capable of mulching down a skyscraper and stopping half a millimeter from the street. At first she had enough to do just to keep up with it. But gradually she met some men, went out with some of them, men who looked good, cared about the arts, had good investments, good hairdressers, strategies for every move. Still, she found she'd rather just go out with Calvin, to clubs where bouncers dressed in gold lamé and caged guys writhed in underwear above their heads.

"Tie me to the mast," Calvin would cry and clutch her arm, Margy dancing in a little patch of open space, no one meeting her eyes, as a solid wall of guys pressed in to rub their butts discreetly against Calvin's. He liked to dress up in a leather tux, with aviator scarf. He liked his lovers beefy and hirsute, two hundred pounds at least, and dumb.

"Oh, God, he's so *inarticulate*," he'd moan into her ear after he'd tried to have a conversation with the biggest guy he could find.

Margy introduced him to her dates sometimes, at dinner in the restaurant of Calvin's choice (nouvelle Japanese, unisex waitpersons with tattoos on their shaved heads), and both of them would listen as the man explained how to choose a life insurance company, or the best tax shelters for the symphony.

"Please kill me," Calvin wrote once on a napkin, handed it to her, and Margy did not see the man again.

～

One day at rehearsal, a rumor ran through all the chairs, eyebrows rising on the most impassive faces. They had just been signed to play a benefit for Russian Jews, and the soloist would be a legendary pianist who rarely played in North America. Michael Sein had won the Chopin Prize when he was just fourteen, and everything since then, even edging out the Russians in Moscow. He was close to forty now, and the *New York Times* had lately said he was the hottest pianist in the world. But he lived reclusively in the south of France and refused to play in public for long periods, except to help the grape farmers, or drought victims in Africa, and never in the States, though he'd grown up in Brooklyn, protégé of a famous New York pianist. No pictures were included on his albums, several of which Margy owned, though other pianists would require the use of an 8-by-10 photograph of them (in black tie, simpering) each time anyone used their names.

"He is not a pretentious guy," the concert master kept explaining to small hushed groups. "He wants everyone to call him Mike. But you've never heard Rachmaninoff till you've heard Sein." He studied the effect on them, bright-eyed. "You've never heard *arpeggios* till you've heard Sein."

Margy listened skeptically. She'd met some legends before now: a flautist who thought he was a lonely man (but was a lecher in disguise), a cellist who had played a recent solo with all the verve of a finger exercise (but when the next one came along, he got that too). A famous bassist had made much of Calvin when he played with them. "You're a real musician, Jim," he said, getting Calvin mixed up with the fellow who played next to him. Now every time he came to town, he cried, "Jim!" and crossed the room to embrace Calvin in front of everyone.

Michael Sein arrived, started to rehearse with them. At first he looked entirely unremarkable. Short and stocky, in an old cardigan and beat-up tennis shoes, he hunched over the keys, nothing of him showing but his hair, long black-and-silver curls springing up. The visiting conductor had him play through one time by himself, Rachmaninoff number two. Fingers gently crushing keys, every hammer ringing like a temple bell, he subtly swelled the sound till it was oceanic, stunned the air. When he finished, and sat with head drooped toward the keys, musicians all across the stage slammed down their feet and clacked their bows on music stands. Then he lifted up his head.

A prickling surge rushed over Margy's body as her genes stood up to take a look. His large eyes were so pale they were almost colorless, and they inched around the orchestra like beams of pure intelligence. They passed over her and looked away. A moment later, he looked again. The blood drained out of Margy's brain. Bending toward the floor, she shuffled through her sheet music as if she'd taken out the wrong page.

"I heard you play once," he said to her that night, at a party after the benefit. Spotting him across the room, she had retreated to the kitchen, wondering how she would get past him to the elevator door. But a moment later he followed her.

"Years ago, with the Boston Symphony," he went on, low and calm. "I don't remember what it was, but I remember how you played."

She forced herself to look at him. His eyes swam with light, like the fabulous jeweled orbs of a dragon in a cave. They examined every millimeter of her face and hair.

"I grew up in their youth orchestra," she explained. "They were just being nice to me."

His face relaxed in soft lines like a child's. "I don't think that was it. There was a certain quality to how you played, very unusual in a young girl, or an American of any age. Something . . . mysterious. Americans usually want everything explained, everything simple, a simple story about good and evil. But Boston was right, if they heard something else in you."

She changed the subject, asked him where he lived in France. He told her it was a medieval village in the mountains of Languedoc with no electricity or running water. His children had been born there, and he had delivered them himself, assisted by a local midwife all in black. He made no mention of a wife, just said "we" once or twice. Since rehearsal that morning, his hair had been mowed short, but it still tried to curl, in bent blades like trampled grass. A few whorls of hair seemed to grow from his earlobes, floating toward his shoulders like prayer curls, and Margy furtively examined them. But even they looked beautiful to her.

"I need someone to talk to," he said, looking into her eyes. "Someone like you, who answers back. We must see each other often. We will be allies."

Margy went home stunned and couldn't sleep. Next day, everyone talked about him. Desperate dad, they said. His wife had lately left him and moved to Chicago, taking his small sons. That was why he had agreed to play with them. His wife was from an old Chicago family, beautiful, the rumor said, taller than Michael, and a snob, named Carter Arlington. He was coming to Chicago now as often as he could, camping in a studio across the street from his wife's place in Lincoln Park and sharing custody.

Two days after the benefit, Margy passed him on a street near her apartment, with his little boys, holding their hands. They were maybe three and five, tender, serious, alert, and when they saw their father watching Margy cross the street, they stretched up on their toes to look at her, necks as delicate as flower stems.

~~

"A nice man," she said to Calvin when he asked, despite the shrewd look he was giving her. She did not see Michael again that spring, though she often went for walks in the park near his block. A few months later, he sent her two postcards, one from Languedoc and one from Paris, where he'd played a benefit ("Rachmaninoff again. I thought of you").

And in the fall he came back to play with them, five concerts of Tchaikovsky, Mussorgsky, Prokofiev, and Borodin, all in his dazzling way. In rehearsal, everyone she talked to seemed a little bit in love with him. She was only one of them, another starstruck junior violinist, nothing more.

After his first concert, she loitered as she changed out of her slinky blacks, hoping not to see him in the hall, until the locker room was empty and lights were starting to go out. But when she finally emerged, he was still there, talking to the concert master near the stairs, and he stepped into her path with unexpected speed.

"Are you in a hurry? Can you talk? Have coffee, maybe, or a beer?"

She drove him up to Lincoln Park in the aged Volkswagen convertible she'd lately bought, with a windshield that iced up from the inside in wintertime, and stopped off at a former speakeasy, where Renaissance paintings were grainily projected onto screens and the tape deck played a scratchy loop of the late Romantic repertoire. Michael ordered pints of ale and scrutinized her face.

"Tell me everything about your life," he said, smiling. "Are there men who hate you because you broke their hearts? Are there men you haven't seen for years but still think of? What are you afraid of most? What do you love?"

Margy vibrated as she watched him, strong hands that had mesmerized a thousand people earlier that night resting on the table, cuffs pushed up exposing hairy wrists. She tried to think of things she loved. Italian shoes and Japanese jazz. Caillebotte and Chagall, Camus. Puccini, Beethoven, Rachmaninoff. Venice, Florence, parts of France.

"I love Languedoc," she cried, a sudden rush of feeling overcoming her, though all she could remember of the place was a wash of sun in a café, a beach with white-rock mountains rising cool behind. Half delirious, she cast about for something more to praise, and landed on a city two hundred miles away. "I love the Gaudis in Barcelona. I love Picasso. I love cassoulet!"

Michael watched her, eyes alight. He plucked a strand of fuzzy hair out of her face, precisely, not touching the skin.

She was too shy to ask him much, except about his music and his children, neutral things. A few facts he volunteered. As a kid he had been bored with school, rode the subway to Manhattan and picked pockets on Fifth Avenue, masquerading once when caught as a war orphan from Germany, parents killed in concentration camps. When he got tired of that, he learned to put the wallets back into the pockets where he found them, or chase the victim down and hand it back, refusing a reward.

"Wallets are too easy," he said. "I decided to go after bigger things. Some of them are actually too easy too."

"Like what?"

He pressed his lips together, as if satisfied. "Another time. I'm afraid I must be off now, home. I'll walk from here."

"I'll take you," she said, startled, unwilling to let him go.

He looked at her gently. "All right."

She knew exactly where he lived, having looked him up in the phone book. But he directed her to the block before his own.

"This is my corner," he said intensely. "Is it? *Yes!*"

She stopped the car, but he made no move to leave, and they talked another hour in the dark.

~

She made no plans with Calvin after the rest of Michael's concerts. But after the next three, he disappeared before she came out of the locker room. On the day of his last one, an early snow began to fall, and by evening it had turned into a blizzard. The concert was not canceled, and they played to a diminished crowd, the hall smelling of wet wool and cold snow. Even sealed inside, they could feel the silence past the walls, piling on the roof, and they played more subtly, every note a trespass in a quiet deep as sleep.

When it was over, and she was suited up in jeans and boots, Michael was in the hall. Without a word he touched her arm, and she quickly turned, walked close beside him past assorted members of the orchestra, up the stairs, and out the door.

Streets and buildings had been smothered under snow. Not a vehicle was moving on the avenue, quiet as a country field, mounds of white gleaming over a hundred cars abandoned in midstreet. Snow was still coming down, straight and fast and silent, and streetlights lit it from above in high white domes, like ghostly Arcs de Triomphe in the windless air.

"It could be Paris!" Margy cried, bounding through the drifts, dangerously happy to be out with him. "That's where we are, in Paris, from this minute on!"

It was no use trying to drive. Instead they tracked across fresh fields of six-lane thoroughfares, snow leaking in their boots and clumping in their eyelashes. Bearlike in his army jacket, Michael humped along in meditative, bobbing strides, as if he thought the act of walking were a touch ridiculous. Here and there a taxi skidded by, and one began to spin, graceful, in slow motion, like ballet for cars.

"It's like *Fasching*," Margy said. "Or Mardi Gras or *carnaval*, all the rules suspended for a night. Why don't we do that in this country, ever? Except when there's a flood, or the Cubs win the Series?"

Dancing ahead, she spun around, dropped to her knees in the snow, and flung glittering handfuls into the air, letting them sift coldly down on her.

"Don't you hate rules? Brush your teeth! Love your neighbor! Three-four time!"

Michael ploddingly caught up with her. "Rules are good. Without them, we would never feel like this."

Margy looked up, laughed breathlessly. *We*, he said. *We* feel like this. She stayed on her knees, hands full of snow.

"You mean it feels so good when they stop? Thanks very much. I'll take the feeling, hold the masochism."

"No, you won't, because you're a musician, and you know."

Pulling off his gloves, he started brushing snow out of her hair, gently, with a musing face, as if not noticing what he was doing.

"The end result may sound like bursting into song, but you know you spent a year on the fingering. Where would the passion be without the three-four time?"

Shivering at the feel of his hands, she stayed on her knees until he stopped. Slowly she stood up in front of him, champagne explosions in her body sharpening to sting. He looked down at her coat, and seemed to study it.

"Look at you. You're a mess."

Smiling slightly, as if amused at himself, he began to brush the snow off, lightly touching through the heavy wool with his bare fingertips all down the front of her, as if she were his wife, or his child.

～

He hailed a cab that night and put her in it by herself. He disappeared, and did not write to her. She tried to practice, tried to sleep. The season had only just begun, and she had to be on top of at least three pieces every week, some of them world premieres, tough contemporary works commissioned for the CSO and new to everyone. For one she had to learn to land on sixteen double-stops in nine measures, while playing out of sync with the row in front of her. For another she had to meet with just the strings to practice flipping down their bows to rap them on the music stands, then up to stroke on the next beat, over and over like a squadron of baton twirlers. She had rehearsal almost every day, concerts half the nights, and practice the remainder of the time.

One Sunday morning in December, she opened the *New York Times,* and Michael was on the cover of the magazine. On a bench by a grand piano, in his usual old cardigan, he had flashed the camera a blazing look, and there it was. Feverishly she read the article. *World-Class Pianist, Ultra-Private Life, Devoted Family Man.* Pictures of him with his kids. Quotes from things he'd said. Yes, he liked Rachmaninoff, but in general he preferred the older repertoire.

"Imposing formal restrictions on a piece is like monogamy," he'd told the interviewer. "All of us have lots of erotic opportunities. But I restrict myself to only one, for the sake of order, and for certain emotional benefits. In music, the point of departure is always the maximum degree of passion. But the control has to be there too, to make it sing. You only hear the sweetest songs when you're listening through barbed wire."

Agitated, Margy paced the apartment, read the quotes again. Did he feel he had to say this to her, in a public newspaper? Was he back together with his wife? She searched the article, but did not find a single word about his marriage.

It could not hurt, she decided, to write him a note, let him know she understood. Getting out paper and pen, she didn't have to think about what to say. She wrote fast, as if in a trance, crossing nothing out.

"Of course you're right," she wrote. "The point of departure is always a maximum degree of passion, and we think we accept the restrictions with regret. But in fact they may enhance the passion, and a person who devotes her life to music may be in love with exactly that. It's thrilling to know how well you see this, though it makes me feel a little naked."

Even the wildest break with form still made up its own rules, she noted blandly at the end, and mentioned her favorite Japanese jazz musician. Did Michael know his work? Sealing the letter in an envelope, she addressed it to his place in Chicago, walked it to the corner mailbox, dropped it in.

Hours later, as she was practicing, a thought passed over her. What was that she had written to him? "Naked," "thrilling," "in love." Had she said that? She held her breath, and saw an image of her body leaping from the window.

She shook the image off. Michael had said they would be allies. He would understand.

~~

Months went by without a reply, through winter into spring. On a warm May afternoon, she stepped onto a busy street near her apartment, and realized that Michael was walking toward her in the crosswalk, with a young blond woman she had never seen.

"The answer is no," he called as soon as he saw her. "What was the question?"

Margy felt her body blush down to the toes.

"Never mind," she said, and walked past them fast, the blond girl watching her. She was about eighteen, leggy in a short black dress and long blond ponytail.

"No, no!" his voice behind her called out urgently. "What was it? Please! I just can't remember."

Reaching the curb, Margy looked back. Rooted in the middle of the street, he stood holding out his arms. Above his head the orange signal flashed, WAIT, WAIT. Quickly she yelled back the stupid question she had asked, about the Japanese jazz musician.

"Ah," he called, nodding. "That's right." Waving pleasantly above his head, he turned and walked away with the blond.

A baby-sitter, she decided late that night, tossing in her bed. Why hadn't she thought of that? He had talked about how hard it was to find them, and how he looked with avaricious eyes at every young person he met, wondering how they'd be with his kids. She got up, read his interview again. He was a good man, serious and fatherly. She believed in him.

A few weeks later, on a hot June afternoon, she was staring at a pile of kumquats in the fruiterer's, too depressed to imagine eating anything, when she felt a sudden tingling down her skin. There he was an inch away, examining her as if she were a rare and beautiful object. In a panic, she tried to turn away. *(Thrilling. Naked. The answer is no.)* But his fingers closed on her bare arm as furtively he checked the store.

"Come with me. I know a spot."

He led her to a tall grove in the park, where they sat on the grass with their shoes off, both of them in shorts, bare legs an inch apart. They talked for three hours, about music and musicians, who they knew.

"So who are your lovers anyway?" he demanded. "Any pianists I know? I bet some of them are conductors."

"No, nobody," she said and blushed. "No lovers at all."

He glanced at her skeptically, but then relaxed, seemed re-assured. He looked thinner, in a polo shirt with a hole in one sleeve, his limbs as graceful as a boy's. His eyes crept over her. When a leaf soared from a tree and landed in her hair, he extracted it and smoothed the place where it had been, fingers lingering.

～

"Piano envy," Calvin said. Margy had once wanted to be a pianist herself, take up the whole stage instead of droning in the background with the other violins, like bees in an orchard on a summer afternoon. But her hands had always been too small.

"Any *famous pianists* in here?" he said archly, coming into her apartment, and cast his eyes around. They were going to a used-clothing store to pursue his lifelong search for a propeller beanie and an intact pair of spats. Margy had on a dress with a short skirt, and he eyed her skeptically.

"Your thighs are the most Venusian part of you," he said. "But best to keep them covered up. For the mystery, you know." Taking hold of her skirt, he tugged it firmly down.

She started seeing his therapist, but he only wanted to talk about her father, and the next one she tried sat in frozen Viennese silence for three months. Finally she found a woman whom she liked, and they went over all the possibilities. Masochism, poor self-image, guilt. Freud was just no help. He always accused some young woman of being in love with an older man. That was the reason why she'd lost the use of her right arm, or fallen mute, and if she'd just admit it, she'd be fine. But Margy *knew* she was in love with Michael Sein.

"I'm in love with Michael Sein," she said, over and over, lying on the couch. It didn't seem to help.

~~

In February, he came back to play with them again, and he was suddenly less popular with the symphony. Rumor had it that he'd tried to change the program he would play.

"A certain manipulative bastard," was how the concert master now referred to him, and everyone knew who he meant.

Michael waited for her after each rehearsal and concert, and they went out for lunch or dinner or a beer. He also asked to see her now on other nights, took her to an opera or a play. Sitting next to him in a dark hall, the space between their shoulders charged like electrons inside a bomb, she hardly noticed what was happening on stage. But every evening ended the same way. They parked a whole block from his home and talked another hour in the dark.

"Maybe he's gay," Calvin said, eyebrows wiggling up and down. "Maybe I should give him a call?"

He still had never said a word about his wife, though he often spoke with delight about his children. Margy didn't ask, sure that he would talk about his marriage when he wanted to.

Once when he said "we," she blanked out for a moment, and asked, "Who?"

"Carter," he said slowly, a look of wonder on his face.

"Oh," said Margy, trying not to feel dumb.

A few nights later, as she arrived at Orchestra Hall, he was being dropped off in a new Lincoln. The driver was only a dark shape inside, but even yards away Margy could hear her yell at him in a high and furious voice.

"You don't have to tell me that. You think you can just—"

The shouting swelled as Michael stepped out of the car, dimmed as he slammed the door. Meditatively he bobbed away, not looking back. A moment later he noticed Margy, and his face lit with delight.

"See you afterward?" he said, tipping back his head to beam into her eyes.

She dreamed that she was trying on his wife's wedding ring, and Michael saw her and did not mind. She dreamed they ran away in a Volkswagen van, pursued by guerrillas, escaped across an open sewer on rusty pipes. When they made it to the other side, Michael leaned his face down close to hers.

"Yes, we're going to kiss each other," he said, and Margy was so happy, she woke up.

~~

That summer, Michael played in the CSO's festival at Ravinia, a few miles north of Chicago, a mixed program of Bach, Stravinsky, Brahms, only for one night. He appeared at rehearsal on his own but asked Margy to eat with him on break, and they found a little Russian place, then walked along the lake. He seemed disturbed, fists plunged in the bulged-out pockets of a worn linen jacket, and he lectured her about what was wrong with the orchestra, the music industry.

"I hate managers and agents and other money-grubbing Philistines. I hate the twentieth century. I refuse to care about money," he said and glared at her as if she'd said he should. "I hate property, the way it governs the Western imagination. Everything we think is trapped inside of it."

He stared down at her ankles, bare in summer flats. Blue-green veins were visible beneath her skin.

"Do you have on *stockings?*" he demanded.

"No, nothing."

He looked at her resentfully.

"But that's what you are, aren't you. A blue stocking."

They drove back to Ravinia, and Margy changed into her summer concert whites, feeling drained. She leaned against a wall offstage, waiting to go on. When Calvin came out of the dressing room in a crisp white jacket and bow tie, he took one look at her and started kneading her neck. Margy leaned against him, eyes closed, and when she looked up, Michael was coming down the hall toward them, glaring above their heads.

"What is happening with you and Little Lord Fauntleroy?" he hissed beside her ear the moment he had played his encores, bowed his bows. "What does he think he's doing, anyway?"

She suddenly felt mean. The tail of something cold lashed her. Usually they stepped outside to talk, for privacy, but she turned down the hallway toward the crowded dressing rooms.

"Aren't you worried about walking so close to me?" she said, hardly moving her lips. "Aren't you afraid someone will tell your wife?"

Half the orchestra watched them, but Michael's hand shot out and gripped her wrist. Veering in one swoop, he pulled her out the side exit. The moment they were alone, he let go.

"You like to torture me, don't you," he said, and strode away into the dark.

It was a warm and windy night, bright lights wavering, trees surging in the wind, as the crowd streamed toward their cars, taillights blazing red in the lots. Michael walked fast the other way, and she caught up with him under loud, gyrating trees.

"Are you going back to France?" she said calmly. Gravel crunched under their feet.

He didn't answer. So she described the trip she planned to take to Italy, in August, with Calvin.

"Jesus, it's just like I said!" he gasped, and looked at her, eyes wild. He turned his face away.

"August is a lousy time to go," he said spitefully. "Too hot, and not a single concert anywhere, not even an opera, in the country that invented it. Do you realize that?"

Margy was so tired she felt blasé. "Yes, I realize that. Well, I'm going home. Good night."

She knew it meant she wouldn't see him again this time. She turned and started walking toward her car. Little pieces of Chicago blew into her eyes, road grit and flakes from people's shoes. He followed her. When they got to the car, he stood beside her while she unlocked it. He stared away, as if he hated the sight of her.

"Well, look me up if you're in Italy," she said pleasantly, opening the door.

Michael's icy eyes came suddenly alive in the streetlight, black dots of the pupils like bullets aimed at her.

"I never look you up now. What makes you think I would then?"

All the air rushed out of her. Getting into the car, she slammed the door.

Michael pounded on the window, waited till she opened it. Awkwardly, he took hold of her wrist, looked down.

"Tell me where you'll be and how to get in touch with you. I suppose I might come to Italy."

〜

August sun lay panting on the deck of their hotel, waterside by the canal, as randy whiffs of Venice blended with the coffee and the rolls. Calvin was pouting this morning, in a three-piece linen suit, no shirt, and silk necktie knotted loosely around his bare neck. She kept her voice low, underneath the rippling of water all around. She didn't think the waiters spoke English, but you never knew.

"Calvin, relax. We did not make love. You don't have to punish me."

Calvin gave her a disdainful glance and looked away.

"A little less pocket psychology, please."

She reached for the butter, and he slapped her wrist.

"You're going to get fat, you know. And do you realize you're twenty-*six* years old? Practically stale goods. I wouldn't turn down any more fabulous offers if I were you."

They had chosen this hotel for its old-world touches, despite the old-world plumbing moaning in the night, the old-world mattresses, and when a waiter slid toward them, damask towel over one arm, silver salver in the other hand, they stopped to watch. The waiter was in his fifties, tall and upright with the face bones of a god, and a dignity that disapproved of young Americans.

"*Signora, per lei,*" he said, and bowed under their deck umbrella, ignoring the sultry look Calvin had fixed on him.

On the salver was a blue-edged telegram. Margy folded it into her hand. Suddenly the sunlight on the water glinted painfully through her dark glasses. She rose to thread between the tables as Calvin called behind her plaintively.

"Oh, don't start being mysterious at this late hour of the day."

In the cool dark of the marble lobby, the telegram was a black page. She stared at it until the words emerged.

"Coming to Venice, looking you up. Hotel Orchidea, 3 P.M."

~~

Michael's room was on the highest floor, windows arched above a tight canal. He'd left them open to the baking sun, and anyone across the way could watch them where they lay, as heat shimmered above the bed and a breeze raised little hairs along the curve of Michael's back, moving under Margy's hands. In the canal below, water sighed and slapped. Yellow sunlight crept across the floor and up the stucco wall. Margy tried to memorize each moment, yet she wanted them to end, so they could talk. They had so much to say.

"We haven't much time," was all he had said before, and it was true. Her flight home was only days away, and what would they do then? She wanted to tell him how she had suffered, hear him say the same. When he first leaned over to kiss her, standing by the window of his room, she cried out.

"I've had dreams in which you did that!" she tried to say. But his tongue was reaching down her throat, as if trying to devour her.

The light grew smoky red, like a blush along the tiered fronts of houses across the canal. Michael lay half over her, smelling not at all like Henry Bergstrom (soap, deodorant, cologne). Instead he smelled like musk and sweat, much more exciting to her nose. His chest was furred with silky hair. Asleep, his face looked artless and naive. Suddenly the eyelids rose, and there he was, assessing her.

He stretched, rolling off. "That was quite a note you wrote to me."

Her face went hot. "I was hoping you'd forget that now."

He smiled. "No, no, it was priceless. I wouldn't have missed it for anything. Do you always come on like that?"

"Always?" she said, still too languid to lift her head.

"With your other lovers."

She smiled. "Oh, yes, my million men."

"I suppose I know some of them?" he persisted. "They're mainly musicians, aren't they?"

She wrinkled her nose at him. "Oh, sure. And yours? All musicians?"

He frowned. "No need to talk about that. But really, do you always have to pretend it's love, like Tristan and Isolde?"

She sat up. "Pretend it's love? I haven't been pretending. I haven't been to bed with anyone for years."

He glanced at her, concerned. "But that's so ascetic!"

"That's not *ascetic*. I only wanted you, is all."

She felt ashamed. Everything she said seemed so naive. Clutching the sheet around her, she tried to cover herself, gradually hearing what he'd said before.

"Do you mean to say, you had the nerve to think I was in love with you, when I only wrote you that—"

"No, no!" he broke in. "Not until after I said no to you."

She stood up, trailing the sheet. Postcoital aggression on this level was a new one, but she could handle it. At the window, sheet secured around her like a strapless gown, she studied the dark houses across the way until she felt more calm.

"Yes, and wasn't that an ascetic thing to do, saying no to me? Haven't you denied yourself too, because of your kids? And whatever it is that happened to your marriage," she added, stepping gingerly into this new territory.

Michael's face contracted with amusement in the gloom.

"My marriage. My wife, as you always call her, as if we were good burghers going to church. Not everyone is so conventional."

She steadied herself on the window arch. In the sky outside, the last pigeons winged home to San Marco. A rim of gold gleamed on a dome she didn't recognize.

"So you're not married after all?"

He leaned back on the pillow, spread his arms.

"The last romantic. It's not a property arrangement between us. We keep money out of it, and we don't own each other's bodies. You could have found that out a long time ago, if you'd asked. But you don't ask questions, do you? I realized that a while ago, when we were screwing. You don't know anything about me."

"Rules, you said. Rules are good. You have lots of erotic opportunities, but you restrict yourself to only one."

He chuckled. "What a memory you have. But it was just a metaphor, a very effective one, I see, since you remembered it."

She found the silky yellow sundress she had put on eagerly that afternoon. Her flesh felt dead inside it, and she lashed it on like a bandage. From the bed, Michael watched, looking contemplative.

"Listen. I want you to know that I've been touched by this passion you've developed for me. But you should realize it has nothing to do with me. It has to do with things you have no control of. The idea you have of me is a fiction."

She looked for her underpants, her sandals, her barrettes, all lost on the dark floor.

"And yours of me is not?"

"It wouldn't be gailant to say no."

His voice was quiet, reasonable, in the dark.

"Tell me, did you get along with your father? Was he frequently absent when you were small? You must realize that's the reason why you fall in love with strangers and write them revealing notes."

Margy stood still. "And for you it has been?"

He let a thoughtful pause go by.

"Tolerance," he said. "Tolerance, and a willingness to give people what they seem to want, if I like them."

"Tolerance!" she shouted. Spit flew from her mouth.

She controlled her voice. "So you think you were not involved?"

"No, no! I don't think that. I was lusting after you, too. And it was very nice."

Reaching from the bed, he tried to take her hand, but she recoiled. He sighed like a parent with a screaming child.

"And I hope it won't be the last time. But, you see, I've been as interested in talking to you as anything, seeing what I can learn from you. This is not the season of sensuality with me. This is the season of intellectual interests."

After a silence, he asked calmly, "How do you meet your men?"

~

The stones of the street were cool below the bare soles of her feet, with the hint of water underneath. She'd found her sandals at the last second, but broke the thong of one in her rush to get away, and now she held them in her hands, stepping blindly down the darker streets. In the lighted squares, she could see groups of men, and she'd learned to stay away from them. She'd been in Rome about ten minutes when the first man had followed her. Sometimes they kept it up for miles, offering her money, saying what they planned to do to her, usually in English, as if they knew she was American, therefore attainable. She bought Italian clothes, pinned her hair up flat. But tonight her barrettes lay somewhere on the floor of Michael's room, with her underpants. Groping barefoot through the dark, she could feel her hair wave in wild curls, the evening breeze like hands beneath her dress, on her naked buttocks, on her sex.

"Blue under the eyes?" Michael had said in the lit hall, catching her chin to peer into her face. It was, he said, a sign of orgasm to the French. Shaking his fingers off, she bolted down the stairs and out the door.

Across a lighted square, she could see the cleft of black that meant the Grand Canal, where there might be gondolas, a *vaporetto* stand. But she had to cross the *campo* first, avoiding several strolling bands of men. Leaving the shadow, she darted toward a tree, and heard a male voice call out gleefully.

"*Ola, cocca!*" it cried, and others quickly answered it.

She dove into an alley, putrid with a reek of fish and urine, landing once on something soft and wet. A man panted behind her now.

"*Tesora mia, carina,*" he moaned, closer every step.

The alley opened on a quay, not far from the spot where Calvin had dropped her off that afternoon. She'd told him her aunt had come to town, and that she'd find her own way back. But now there were no gondolas in sight, except one, tied up at the quay, and it was occupied.

Four shoes scuffed the paving stones behind her now.

"I make you feel like burst melon," one man murmured musically. "I make you scream like cat in heat."

She glanced around for a café, anything with lights. One man put a hand on her arm. She shook him off, but he came back, as if her bare feet were a license, and he could see she'd lost her underpants.

"*Cinquanta mille. Sessanta,*" he hissed into her ear, and boldly gave her buttock one quick stroke.

In the gondola beside the quay, the passenger rose up. It was a figure shrouded all in black, black cape and black three-cornered hat with a white mask, the *bautta* worn by Contarinis and Foscaris and Grimanis centuries before, to slip into each other's bedrooms unannounced, or lug someone to the Canale Orfano in a sack.

"Ahh-eeeeee!" the figure shrieked, spread wide the black wings of its cape, and leaped out of the gondola, landing near them on the paving stones, showing white tennies with no socks. Letting go of Margy, the two men shrank back.

"Unhand that maiden!" the figure cried, taking up a fencing stance, but they already had.

On the way back in the gondola, Calvin rode with one foot on the prow, facing forward like George Washington, still in his cape and mask.

"God, that was exhilarating," he kept saying with a shudder, shoulders back, one hand tucked, Napoleonic, to his diaphragm. He had just had a hunch, he said, like Superman, and waited there for hours at fabulous expense. But it was worth it, every lire.

"Unhand that maiden!" he cried, flourishing his arms inside the cape.

"*Bene, bene,*" said the gondolier behind them, every time.

Leaning on the rail, Margy let her hand trail down into the water, where it was cool and alive. The tide was at its height, and she could feel it flowing in from all the oceans of the world, past rocks and locks and sea walls, over barriers of every kind, swamping the piazza of San Marco ankle deep and seeping underneath the streets to soak the ancient oaks that held the city up, in slow dissolve, until one day the towers would begin to fall, the heavy bells, the domes and marble halls, the lions in gold leaf, all waiting for the flood to rise and float them free.

By the Shining Big Sea Waters

~~~~~~~~~~

Webster grew his hair out long in graduate school, because it made him look less white. Straight, crow-black, it shone like fur and brought out the hawk in his nose. He was in Berkeley at the time, but even in Berkeley men got haircuts now. Students cut theirs shorter every year, streamlined, as if for a quick getaway, and stuck a diamond in one ear. In Berkeley the '60s had died, and rotted. It had happened long ago, when Webster was still setting model planes on fire and shooting them with BBs from a window of his mother's house. He liked to start the fire down in the yard, run inside, and shoot the flaming airplane from upstairs. Once he did it to a model boat, floating and flaming on a bucket full of water, till a well-placed BB sank the boat and put the fire out.

Now he was a sober lab assistant, working for a doctorate in oceanic microbiology. He showed freshmen how to suck sea-urchin sperm into a tube, line the egg up in the scope, add a drop of sperm, and watch. He caught a worm for them, like a live lace ribbon undulating up through water into light, a worm that took four hundred million years to make and would become extinct in their short lives, so they could have hair dryers and disposable pens. When he published his first paper, on the decline of plankton shrimp in intertidal waters, he used a new last name, an Algonquian word that meant "he lives beside the sea." He found it in the only dictionary of that tongue, written three hundred years before by a French baron. Leatherbound, small and thick on rugged parchment, it was made for the saddlebags of lone white men, invading forest trails. Webster had to struggle with the French, the antique script, every *S* shaped like a florid *F.* But he worked it out. *Unutshimakitshigamink,* that was it. Webster Unutshimakitshigamink.

"White man is like the coyote," he explained. "Pisses on his kill, so nothing can eat it, not even him."

In the lab, his friends all stared, waited for him to grin. Most of them had known him and each other since MIT, and the rest of them still worked past midnight as a group, trooped out for pizza late, told jokes from the "Three Stooges."

"Webster, You Nut," they started calling him. "Webster Nutmink, last of the Mohican braves. How, chief." They patted their mouths with open hands. "Who-wa-oo-wa-oo-wa-oo."

Webster worked at his own station, and did not grin. His hair grew long, folded around him like a pair of wings. When he was on his Harley, it would belly out behind him like a sea anchor. In the lab, he braided it and tied it with a leather thong. He told his students about a prehistoric shrew that only ate the eggs of a certain duck. The shrews waxed so successful, they ate every duck egg before it hatched, until the ducks became extinct.

"White man is the shrew that ate the duck eggs till the ducks were gone," he said. "Followed by the shrews."

~

He didn't know how to be an Indian. He'd never met one in Connecticut, when he was growing up. He hadn't even been a Scout, and when he tried to burn his mother's house down at the age of eight, he had to learn fire-building on his own. Making a pile of trash, giggling and trembling, he fumbled with the match. Cereal boxes did not light, he found, but cigarette packets did. Running to the kitchen, he climbed on the counter and took down a carton of Pall Malls. His mother was in the front part of the house, in her office, but when she was in there with a patient she did not come out. She was a psychiatrist, like his father. When Webster was a baby, they'd put him in a Skinner box, which issued him an M&M each time he fitted an odd-shaped block into its corresponding hole, and did not cry.

His parents built the box to teach him what he'd need to know in life, and planned to write a book on how he did. But before the book was done, his mother packed up Webster and drove off into the night, left his father and the box. Her new house was big and cubic, white paint on old wood. When he lit the mound of shredded cigarettes, red packages, and crinkly wrappers, yellow flames shot up and lit the trash, exploded to the eaves, and scorched a wide black triangle of clean white wall. His mother sent him to a specialist in infantile aggression, who watched him while he played with dolls and toy houses.

"Eeeeyaaa*koouum,*" he'd say and make the boy doll kamikaze-dive into the house.

The last time he went east, his mother watched him, eyes merry over the rim of her martini.

"When did you develop this Indian fantasy?" she said.

He didn't try to argue. She must have known about his father's family. They'd lived in Maine three hundred years, and where else would those settlers get their brides? "Jane" or "Rose" they wrote in the family Bible, no last name. They married off their children to the farm next door, where the story was the same: behind the official family tree, a long line of Penobscot or Mohican braves. Native Americans had six hundred languages, but only one blood group, Type O, which Webster shared. His father hadn't even had to shave, his brown skin smooth. He must have plucked the few hairs that grew, the way the Indians did, though Webster'd never asked him while he could. His father had married two more times and had several other children, some of whom Webster had met. After the third divorce, on his sailboat off the coast of Maine, his father had put a bullet through the back of his own throat. Drunk, his mother said, though Webster did not suppose she really knew.

~

Near Berkeley, on the California coast, Miwok had been living just a century before, but now they were all dead, leaving nothing but some piles of clam shells from which even the smell had gone. Once they had had a village in Bolinas, near the reef where Webster did research. He got up at three A.M. and rode from Berkeley in freezing fog to catch a minus tide, when just enough of slippery rock was out that he could crawl and slither half a mile from shore in icy spray, dip his sample jars, and capture a few grams of plankton. Returning as the tide came in, he might plunge to his neck, jars at arm's length above his head, eyes on the next comber that could sweep him off. The reef was huge, long ragged ribs of rock sheltering Bolinas Bay. Miwok had caught fish here in their basket nets for about ten thousand years, and nothing much had happened since to ruin it. It was the biggest, cleanest intertidal zone in North America.

He found a boathouse in Bolinas he could rent. It was on a weathered pier, gray and splintered from salt air, its pilings sunk in the lagoon, a shallow estuary three miles long. The boathouse had no heat, a cold-water shower, and, since the lagoon was just a wide place in the San Andreas Fault, any night the earth might open wide and take it down. But it had water all around, and snowy egrets waded past, while harbor seals hauled out to sunbathe on the sand. Across the lagoon a mountain rose two thousand feet, dark green and silent in yellow light: Tamalpais, sleeping princess to the Miwok. Farther inland you could see her, a curved hip, a sloping flank, her head thrown back and one breast raised, the fire tower on top like a hard nipple. Bolinas would be somewhere between her thighs.

He moved in books and a microscope, a sleeping bag and camp stove. He sold his motorcycle, bought an old, dented, metal canoe, some Navajo blankets, and two pairs of moccasins. He gave up white man's time, the telephone and news, hamburgers and pizza, everything that came in plastic, and throwing out the trash. Miwok had pulled salmon from the streams, hunted antelope and grizzly bear. They ate six kinds of acorns, barnacles, sea urchins, bees, and the occasional army worm. Now the salmon, grizzlies, antelope were gone, and the coast for miles around was national park, everything down to the army worms protected under federal law. Webster bought some sacks of beans and rice, and a book on edible plants.

He learned to paddle the canoe in the lagoon, where it was calm. Soon he could ride through the channel, past surfers on the bay, and out to open ocean, where big swells hissed through claustrophobic beds of kelp, and harbor seals came up to stare at him. Bobbing along the reef, he dragged plankton nets to fill his jars and watched the water on the rocks, waiting for it to rise. He had to paddle back in through the channel with the tide. It came out like river rapids, no way

to get back in until it turned again. He could have bought a
tide chart, but Miwok hadn't needed them. The lowest tide
was later every day, and he could time it by the orange pop-
pies that furled shut as the sun declined, even in fog. Then
skunks began to ripple through the grass like long-haired
caterpillars. Finally the deer came out to browse. He didn't
need a clock.

He took his samples, put them onto slides. *Aurelia aurita*
he was tracking now, the moon jellyfish, through its peculiar
plankton forms. Starting from a single cell, it grew to a fat
many-legged worm, took root as a plantlike polyp, then became a swimming star, until one day its legs arced back and
joined, turning its body inside out to make a medusa the size
of a pinpoint.

No one had ever seen the second change, when the polyp
left the rock, shaped itself into a star—and he hadn't seen it either, but so what? Some secrets nature clearly planned to keep,
like why *Aurelia* had to seem four different animals. Numbers
had plummeted in recent years, and guys on grants from power
companies liked to say that ocean populations varied in natural
cycles, nothing to cause concern. Webster planned to prove
them wrong and write a searing article about global warming,
oil spills, pesticides. *White man, turn back,* he'd say. His only

grant was from a group of old ladies who liked to lie in front of logging trucks. Netting plankton, he ran gentle tests and put them back into the water without hurting them.

～

The days shrank, dark and short. Rain came, thudded on the boathouse roof like gray arrows. Waves smashed at the mouth of the lagoon, too big for a canoe. Webster sat inside the cold boathouse, while icy tide lapped just under the floor. He couldn't work, and he was tired of beans and rice. He'd gather food, that's what he'd do. He set off hiking, plant book in his hand.

After four miles of pastureland, uphill in rain, he reached a fir forest, tangy with humus smells, and not a leaf of miner's lettuce anywhere. He found a spring with watercress, and ate a few handfuls. All right, he'd had his greens. Packing more for later, he still felt hollow as an old snail shell.

Searching, he found a dead log with a rash of mushrooms, fragile neon-orange bells that did not look edible. Color like that on a frog meant it was deadly to the touch. How did Miwok decide which to eat? Someone dies, and then you know. He kept looking.

At the foot of a fir tree, he found two succulent white caps, so fat and crisp he had to pluck one out. Brushing off the dirt, he smelled it—and took a bite. The taste was nutlike with a hint of loam. He could feel the trees around him, suddenly, how tall they were and still. Spitting the pulp into his palm, he wiped his hand off on a fern.

Next day, wolfish with hunger, he hitched over the mountain in the rain and bought a mushroom guide. Twenty-three kinds of tan mushrooms were poisonous, fifteen yellow, nine orange, eighteen brown. Most would make you vomit, some showed you God. One green and three clean white ones destroyed the human liver and put you in the ground.

~~

"Welcome to the dock," his landlady said, bringing him lasagna in aluminum. Webster wrapped his hands around it, still hot. He had never smelled anything so good.

"Thank you," he gasped.

She gave him a steady smile. She was a sexy forty-five, with red hair, eyes that could look eager, bitter, eager in a flash. Her house leaned close to his, and on warm days she liked to lie out topless on her balcony, yards from his bed.

"You know," she said, "you could use my stove if you wanted, or my shower. I have lots of hot water. My door is never locked."

Webster glanced away. The last woman he'd lived with had also slept with his best friend, and a great many unnecessary things had happened then. He'd smashed his hand against a wall and hit a joist. A bone had broken through the skin, and by the time they got him to the hospital, his best friend and Dana had agreed that it was really Webster's fault. He had apologized and cleaned his blood off the wall. Sure, he met women now, and sometimes one of them had made him want to try again. But it never worked out right. He would always want too much, or she would, and the other would tell lies. On the whole, it seemed wiser to just apologize to any woman he met and let it go at that. If he forgot, he had his hand to remind him, two of the knuckles flat for life. He felt them creaking as he clutched the burning foil.

"I'm sorry. I'm sort of starved. Mind if I just go eat this now?"

She gave him a bitter-eager grin, and he scuttled into the boathouse, guilty but too hungry to care.

The lasagna warmed his whole body, out to the fingerprints. It was gone before he thought about the foil. Foil was trash, and how much more had already been shed, plastic wrap around the cheese, Styrofoam under the meat?

Grimly, he scrubbed it flat, spread it on his lab table where he would see it glinting every day. It was the last trash he was ever going to make. He had to eat, that much was clear. But wasn't there some way to do it without despoiling the world?

An old rod hung dusty on the boathouse wall, and he got it down, took the reel apart. He found plastic line in tidepools, combed it out, and learned to splice it so it held. Miwok had felled redwood trees with sharp rocks, split them into planks with elk antler, and built their own houses. They had made needles out of bone and sewn clothes from hides of animals they killed with pointed sticks. Webster'd never felled so much as a sapling, and his flannel shirts and jeans came from cotton mills. But he could maybe do this one thing. Searching the beach, he found a hook and a plastic jar for worms. Patching the stock with driftwood, he oiled the reel with grease from his own skin, until it ran out smooth and stopped on command.

The first time he jammed a worm onto the hook, he flinched. The worm arched and tried to flee, its delicate mucosa burst, cloaca pierced. How did Miwok snap the spines of fish, cut out beating elk hearts, rip off skin? He cast the worm off the dock, so he wouldn't have to look at it.

Two minutes later, when he hauled the hook back in, the worm had been sucked off by the tide. He'd have to find a better spot. Hiking to the nearest beach, he jammed another worm on, flinched, and flung it out into the surf. Waves rushed at him, dark green, simmering with rain, and whisked the hook clean every time.

～

One morning, he woke to a strange sound and realized the rain had stopped. The lid of clouds broke open, revealing slots of blue. Tide rushed out through the channel, swollen with rainwater, brown. Now was his chance. The tide would take him past the waves, nothing to strip his hook, and he'd have a chance at bigger fish, yellowtail, lingcod, bass. Two feet, three feet long or more, cooked on a spit over a driftwood fire, until the skin curled black and crackling.

Knees weak at the thought, he dug new worms and packed his rod. As he let down the canoe, stepped in, the current seized it, spun it toward the mouth of the lagoon. With a shock, he felt the icy water through the metal boat. Even close to the lagoon, it felt like snow.

Waves sprang up, bigger than they looked from shore. He had to paddle hard to make the tops before they broke. No one else was out, not a boat or a surfer or even a gull. Thin silver sunlight glinted on the water, as wind flattened swaths of ocean miles across. White clouds scudded fast enough to watch. By the time he reached the reef, his shins ached with cold in the stiff blue jeans.

He passed the longest spine, narrow black rock beneath the waterline. Out of the shelter of the reef, waves whipped by him, fast as thought, twice as big as any normal day. Surging up and down, showered with cold spray, he paddled till the swells rolled by and did not break. Aiming for the kelp beds past the reef, where the big fish would be, he propped the paddle in his armpit, tried to steady the canoe, while he fumbled for a worm, fingers trembling.

Suddenly the water underneath him dropped away, and he looked up to see a green wall gleaming in the sun. Too late to turn and reach the top, he flailed, rose, popped out into air on the back side, and crashed into the trough. The next one loomed above him right away, and it was bigger, broke before he reached the top, swamped him with frigid foam. Kneeling in icy water to his thighs, another green train on the way, he tried to turn the boat, but it was like maneuvering a pool. Waves came at him one-two-three, feathering along the tops, blocked all view of land when they had passed. Numb hands cupped, he tried to sluice the water out, while he gripped the rod between his knees. Giving up, he turned around the reef and started back, canoe half filled and riding low.

Somehow clouds had sealed the sky, and rain began to pock the swells. The canoe didn't seem to move. At last he could see the inlet to the lagoon. Watching the waves, he picked what seemed to be the smallest set and nosed toward shore, hoping they would push him in.

The first wave lifted the canoe and shrugged it off, with a quick slap that almost knocked him overboard. The next one drew it higher, hung it almost vertical. The bow slid and dove straight in. Metal shone under gray water, as the wave and the canoe rolled over him.

～

He had the vest off by the time his head was out, and the moccasins. His hair dragged around him, sweatshirt heavy as a shroud. He peeled it off, skin so numb the water felt almost warm. Jeans clutched his thighs and knees, a straitjacket each time he kicked. No way to get them off.

The canoe had disappeared, the rod and reel with it. Scanning for them, treading over waves, he felt himself drift.

Something pulled him up a wavefront, out to sea. The beach was no more than a quarter mile away. He could see it dimly through the rain. Aiming for it, he applied himself to freestyle for a while, and lifted his head. He hadn't moved. In fact, he'd drifted farther out. Sighting on the mountain, he could see his motion now, southwest, the way the tide left the lagoon. Of course, it was still running out. He had come back too soon. A merry raft of driftwood chips bobbed toward him, passed, and jetted out to sea.

All right. The thing to do with rips was not to resist them. Go with them, swim their way, until they let you go. The trouble was, he couldn't feel his bones any longer. When he raised his head, something shifted in it like a ton of sand. His heart raced in trills, like birdsong. Hypothermia. Soon he'd start to chatter, unable to think.

Floating, he looked down and let his limbs trail like a jelly-fish. The water below was blackish-green, opaque as rock, and huge. Surfers sometimes disappeared. Their boards washed in, crescent bites incised, three feet wide. The favorite food of great white sharks was harbor seals—but their eyesight wasn't keen. A surfboard, a harbor seal, a guy in jeans all looked pretty much the same. The smaller chunks would sink, feed the chub and then the crabs. As crabshit he'd feed the phytoplankton,

then the zooplankton that ate them, and so on till a cell of him
in some seabass fillet became a man again.

〜

A huge wave lifted him, and he jerked his head up, snorted a
noseful of water. He was still alive. Joining the bottom of the
food chain was more difficult than he'd supposed.

He looked around as swells rolled fast through rain. Cresting one, he tried to see the beach. Instead, he saw a silver
prow, below the surface of a wave. Deep under water, wal-
lowing. The next wave lifted it a little less. How many more
before it sank, and rusted, turned to trash, his trash, on the
biggest, cleanest intertidal reef in North America?

"Oh, no," he said. "Oh, no, no, no."

Thrashing across the water, he seized the gunwales, tried
to haul it up. Diving, he got beneath it, shoved. It was heavy
as a safe and did not move.

A tsunami arrived, rolled over it, and he went with it, fingers clamped onto the metal, though he couldn't see it anymore. He was over, under it, but holding on. If it was going to
the bottom, so was he. It was going to the bottom. Casual as
a whale's fluke, the canoe flicked up and slammed his teeth.
Pain shot to his toes. His sight went white, and he let go.

A long time later, sloshing in the break, a wave delivered him onto the beach. He could feel the hard sand underneath him, and the waves as they ran up his legs, withdrew, surged up again.

Somewhere his canoe was settling and crushing life forms near the reef. He wasn't going to think about it yet. He'd think about it in the spring, when the storms left and wildflowers came up. It didn't mean he'd have to be a white man now, eat all the duck eggs till the ducks were gone. It didn't mean that jellyfish would die so he could have a hair dryer, cheeseburgers in Styrofoam. He could come back, search every square inch of the bay. It might take a while. But it wasn't over yet. Crawling out, he sprawled, an X on sand, and marked the spot.

After the Beep

~~~~~~~~~~

$\mathcal{M}$argy changed her clothes six times. She took her glasses off, put them back on, and studied the effect. If she left them on, it meant she knew about the other women, that he wasn't breaking up with them. If she took them off, it meant she thought she had a chance, though he was six-foot-four and looked like Hiawatha, Strong-Heart, Loon-Heart, wearer of the Magic Mittens, owner of the Magic Moccasins. They were a few miles north of San Francisco, on a cold and beautiful lagoon, and she had come to house-sit for her aunt, on her summer break. She had planned to practice violin and enjoy the famous view. Instead, she watched the boathouse on the dock, where Hiawatha lived. Black hair rippled shining to the middle of his back, which was honed hard as a blade, with smooth brown skin. He had a kayak that he lifted up over his head as if it weighed nothing, set it in the water, paddled out into the surf. She watched women stalk like zombies out his dock, mouths slack with dumb longing. One day he stood and gazed down tenderly at one of them. Margy felt suddenly that she had wasted her life.

"Word to the wise," her aunt had said before she left. "San Francisco men, you know, they're spoiled. There are about a hundred women here for every straight guy, so, hey, why should they settle down? Webster keeps them guessing, let me tell you." Her aunt's husband had left her for a girl their children's age, and her aunt's normal expression was a grin of rage.

Margy left her glasses on and mashed her hair back in a bun. She put on the jeans and leotard she wore to practice violin, and flats. She'd had enough ambition in her life. Now she was ready to relax.

"Relax!" people always said to her, as if she were driving them insane.

"You look good, but you seem to be a very nervous person," the personnel director at the symphony had lately snapped, as if to say that nervous people did not make it on the violin. Her friends gave her books on how to make the mind a perfect pale-peach blank. It seemed to be a way to get you *out* of touch with your feelings. But what had feelings ever done for her?

～

Webster showed up in a wrinkled dress shirt, jacket, tie, saddle oxfords that made his feet look huge. The tie was too short for his big chest, black geese flying on a field of mallard green. Margy felt so nervous suddenly, she thought she might pass out.

"Where did you find that tie?" she cried. "Have you owned it since junior high?" It was an awful thing to say. She felt mortified. Her cheeks flamed.

He looked down, slowly flushed. "I guess it was my dad's. It's the only one I've got."

"It's all right," she almost sobbed, her eyes filling. Oh, Christ, she was in love with him. How could she be? She didn't even know this man.

While they drove, she tried to relax, telling him about Calvin, who would have killed for Webster's mallards probably. Webster directed her to a loud Mexican place in Mill Valley, where she drank sangria much too fast. By the time their chimichangas had arrived, she was quite drunk. It helped her see the secret motions in the restaurant. Women stared at Webster, astonished and electrified. They walked out of their way to pass by him. He didn't seem to notice as he calmly talked about his work on plankton jellyfish. He told her how he'd changed his name and tried to live off the land, making no trash, like his Algonquin ancestors.

"Younutshimawhat?" she said, trying not to grin. "What was it before?"

"Never mind. It isn't my name anymore." He started to smile too. "Oh, all right, if you must know. It was Hale. Webster Hale. Puritan enough for you?"

For a moment they both laughed.

"So how did you do at living like your ancestors, making no trash?"

He shrugged helplessly. "I made more trash that year than ever. It shed off me, no matter what I did. Then I noticed, everyone who does this kind of work lives on some pristine beach, and all of us complain about our fellow men, the ones who're ruining the pristine beach. Now I want to finish up my project and get out of here. I want to go live in some city where I can't hurt anything. I *dream* of cities now." He gave her a long, slow stare. "I can't believe I lived without music until you got here."

Margy tipped back her head and smiled. That must be the stare that made those other women lose their minds. His voice alone should be enough to warn off anyone. It was an urgent tenor, Pinkerton, not Sharpless, the baritone, the one that you could trust. A tenor with a voice like that would get the girl, betray her, wind up sorry when she's dead.

"I'm sorry if it bothers you," she said.

He leaned in closer to her, stared into her eyes. "Don't you get it? You are one great violinist. Would you please leave the windows open when you play?"

"Not great," she said quickly. "Just competent."

It said so on her annual reports: 'Competent and versatile, but too nervous. Needs to relax.'

She asked about his childhood, if he rode bareback on the lone prairie.

"The only horses I ever got on were the wooden ones in Central Park, the ones that go around and around. The only adults I ever knew were into Freud. If you have, say, a little re-action formation you'd like to talk about, just let me know. You see, I'm not the savage that you think. I even played piano for a while."

"Not piano," Margy groaned. "I've never known a pianist who didn't break my heart."

Webster's eyes went slightly crossed. "I swear I never learned a thing, except 'Chopsticks' and 'Moon River' with one hand. I can't even whistle on key. Okay, I did once play

'The Moonlight Sonata' for a whole summer. Does that mean I have to break your heart?"

She started to laugh, and tears slid down her cheeks.

They split the check and went to find the film they'd picked, a revival of a heartwarming French comedy about a woman who accidentally has sex with her teenaged son. Margy had seen it several times, and she whispered to Webster, giggling, on the best lines.

"*Royaliste,*" the son says, when asked if he is liberal or conservative.

"'*Royaliste,*'" she whispered next to Webster's ear, so close his hair brushed her cheek. He smelled like warm sand, sun, a week on a Greek isle. Okay, she'd go to bed with him. Why not? A summer romance, light as a French film. After that, she'd watch the girls walk out his dock, and Webster leave with them, and—and—wave lightly, since they were just friends.

She sat up, pushed her glasses up her nose, and tried to pay attention to the film. But it seemed poignant now, the mother desperate for love, as if she hadn't many chances left, when she was only thirty-two. Margy was twenty-eight. In the dark, she smiled until her cheeks began to ache.

〜

Driving back, she tried to start laughing again.

"Don't you love the French? The way they do the cancan up to the abyss?"

He answered fast, out of the dark side of the car, as if he had been waiting to be asked. "Have you ever seen a French movie that wasn't making fun of something like incest or adultery? That great comic subject, betrayal? Almost as funny as suicide."

She let out her air. "Oh, well. It isn't necessary to be serious all the time, is it?" She laughed, to let him see how unserious she could be. "I mean, doesn't it make a difference how you take it? Sometimes it's a joke."

She felt shellacked, encased in plastic. She could not get out. It wasn't safe to stop talking. She mentioned several of her favorite movies, *Cousin, Cousine, Discreet Charm of the Bourgeoisie, Rules of the Game*.

"The French aren't puritans, like us, and we only pretend to be. I mean, we do the same things here, don't we? We just don't talk about it. There's as much betrayal here, only less honesty."

Look at you! was what she meant. *Some puritan.* She wanted to sound light and teasing, French.

In the silence that followed, he seemed to cloud up next to her. Gloom filled the car. The radio picked up Tchaikovsky's Concerto No. 1, the great concert by Horowitz in the dark days of World War II. When it was clear he wasn't going to answer her, she turned it up and sang along, the phony Broadway words.

"'Oh, what exciting moments we share when we're all alone at last!'"

The music lasted while they crested the mountain and descended into fog along the sand.

"Thank you for a lovely evening," she said at her door and offered him her hand. Webster looked down, not taking it.

"Charmed, I'm sure," he said and walked away.

~

She paced the house, too tense to sit. The way he walked away from her, as if *she* were the one with all the lovers, flaunting them! We do the same things here, she had said. Surely he didn't think she meant herself? That was absurd! It was insane!

Charging from room to room, she ran a hot bath, put on Pavarotti and Freni—"*Che gelida manina*"—and scrubbed all trace of chimichangas from her skin. Drying off, she put on a heavy white silk robe that was suitable for Harlow or Garbo. It had been her mother's once, and it was too big for her, but she rolled up the sleeves. This was who she was, a nervous runt who loved only the opera, Tchaikovsky, her dead mother, and her friends.

Picking up the phone, she tapped in Calvin's number. He was in New York this summer, with his twin brother, and it was three A.M. there, but he always said to wake him up if she so much as had a bad dream. When other people gazed over her head, Calvin peered into her eyes and asked her how she was *really*. She didn't know his brother well, and she was jealous of the way they were attached. Woody was also gay from birth, and they seemed not just identical but Siamese.

Their machine picked up.

"Hope you have the taste of joy in your innocent mouth. Just remember, you never know where that joy has been." It sounded like Calvin but might have been Woody.

She cleared her throat and tried her husky alto. "'I'm through with love, I'll never fall again. Through with love—'"

Beep, said the machine and cut her off.

Startled, she almost shrieked. Even machines misunderstood her suddenly. Had she vanished, out here in this vacant place? She was misunderstood. *Maligned*.

She had to make sure Webster knew. She tried dialing 411 (*younutshimawhat?*), but of course he wouldn't have a phone. Ruining the pristine beach!

Down the stairs, she burst barefoot onto the dock, trailing the heavy robe. Wood slats sprang back as she stepped on them and propelled her toward his door. The boathouse was dark, a shadow on black water. She didn't care. She knocked.

"So, it's like this," she said as he stood almost naked in baggy shorts that gleamed whitely in the gloom. *His bones are very long*, she thought. Extensions everywhere, in shins and thighs, a waist that tapered down to flat and then continued on. Wide chest, long arms and hands, as they reached out to pull her up to him.

"I live in Chicago, you live here," she gasped.

"Not right now," he said against her ear and stretched out a long foot to close the door.

~

They lay like bodies washed up on the sand, in his bed, her bed, on the floor. She seemed to have a different body, with an effervescent glow. She couldn't think of anything except his skin. There was a hollow under his shoulder that fit her cheek. Lapsing unconscious there, she drooled on it. This must be what infants felt, nursing. She dreamed the ground opened and he fell into the crack. She tried to grab him, but he woke her up.

"Why are you hitting me?" he said and laughed.

"I was trying to save you!"

"You were *hitting* me. On the chest, like this." He showed her with his fist.

"No," he said when she tried to move away. "You don't just get up afterward. This is part of it too."

He held her, lying on his back with his big feet up. Slender at the heels, they gradually splayed out, widening to long, pre-hensile-looking toes. He pressed his forehead into hers.

"I can see a tiny Webster in your eyes," he said. "And he has this monstrous nose."

But it wasn't monstrous, it was perfect, like the rest of him. He liked to bring her tea in bed, fetch socks for her when it was cold, cook, and do the dishes. Once when she left him alone in her aunt's house, he vacuumed it. Once he caught a huge seabass and baked it hours after it was caught. It was the best meal of her life. He brought his microscope to show her plank-ton jellyfish, beautiful veiled forms that soared across the light, graceful as the dancing hippos in *Fantasia*. He read to her out loud, about the history of pencils, the way the Greeks had practiced medicine. He started reading up on the human wrist, hoping to help her be the world's first pain-free violinist.

"When do you turn into a vampire?" she asked.

"Oh ye of little faith," he said and gave her a back massage when she had finished practicing.

~~

One afternoon while he was out, a beautiful brunette strolled out along the dock and into the boathouse. She had smooth hair sculpted to move with her when she walked, and big breasts pushed up in a tight bandeau, body rolling free as if to say *men want me.*

"Who is that sexy brunette you see?" she asked when she saw him next.

His face went neutral. "I guess you mean Dana."

"An old friend?"

"We used to live together. I see her once a week or so."

Some sort of awful hormone roared through Margy.

"Okay. That's good to know."

It wasn't actually betrayal, was it, if they told you from the start? She decided not to watch the dock when she was practicing. One was enough.

~

She gave him a phone and answering machine, because how else could they conduct a civilized affair in 1982? He called her when he wanted to come over, and most nights he did. One night, she didn't see him leave, but the boathouse lights were off. She called to check. He wasn't home.

"This is a machine," his taped voice said, deep and calm.

She ate alone, tried not to watch for the boathouse lights. When the phone rang, she dove for it.

"Hey, Pappagena," said Calvin's voice.

The downward lurching in her chest made it hard to hear. When she could, Calvin was saying someone—Woody?—had been sick. He couldn't shake the flu and had a strange blood count.

"It's probably nothing. I'm going to make him eat his broccoli. You should see the guy, like some Victorian lady with the vapors. It may be love. I introduced him to this hunk who plays the piccolo, you know, and the guy had tattoos on his *neck* and about a three-pound ball hung from his lower lip. How he gets the embouchure, nobody knows. It was too much for poor Woody. I may have to have him exorcised."

She stretched the cord to reach the window. Still dark on the dock. What was Webster doing right that second? He liked to make love every night, and in the morning too.

"Why don't you both come out here, lie around the beach?" she said dreamily. "It's not real warm here, but it's packed with gorgeous guys."

Calvin sounded impatient. "Hey, you're not listening, are you? Woody is a bit too sick to fly all over the country. He has to see his doctor about twice a day. What are you doing out there, anyway? Boffing Hiawatha?"

It was just a lucky guess. She'd only mentioned Webster once. She didn't tell her love life anymore to Calvin, who used any fact she told him as a long needle for prodding her.

"Paul Bunyan," she said. "Johnny Appleseed."

Calvin chuckled. "I knew it, you saucy wench. He's not a pianist, is he?"

When they hung up, silence boomed through the house. She called Webster again, no luck.

Suddenly, without meaning to be, she was on the dock. The boathouse door was never locked. Inside, she flicked on his light. She hardly had to look.

A plate of homemade brownies sat on his lab table, still fresh. "Happy Birthday, Pooka" was inscribed inside a vegetarian cookbook in lavender ink, with a heart dotting the i. "Love Always, Dana." A single earring lay under the bed, long, dangling, of beaten copper flakes, the kind that tinkled when you walked. Margy had never even pierced her ears. You couldn't play the violin with something flapping from your lobes.

She went home, took a tranquilizer, tried to sleep. She woke up every hour until dawn, but the boathouse lights did not come on.

The next night, he showed up, cheerful and relaxed. Every few minutes as they cooked, he put his arms around her or nuzzled her ear.

"Hey, I'm *trying* to do something here," she said and squirmed away.

They made love that night, and in the morning, and went on that way for a week, until he disappeared again. Margy couldn't even practice violin. Her whole body hurt. Why did she fall in love like this, with men who never would love her?

One morning he stayed late with her, making love a second time. Yellow sun shone on the sheets, windows open to cool, salty air. A voice called just below, "Baby?"

The voice was fruity, sexy, the way Dana walked. Webster stopped moving, gripped Margy's shoulders as if to silence her, though she wasn't making noise.

"Where are you, babe?"

The boathouse door swung open with a groan, Dana's sandals scuffing as she sauntered in. Webster kept his face pressed into Margy's neck as their sweat dried.

~

"Can you get here?" said Calvin's voice.

It was August and the middle of the night, Margy startled out of sleep on Webster's chest. Woody now had meningitis and had suddenly gone into a steep decline. Calvin's voice was bleak.

"His heart stopped a while ago. But they tortured him and brought him back."

"No, wait," she gasped.

Webster had told her how, when he was nine years old, he had tried to bring dead birds to life. Using two extension cords, severed with their wires exposed, he had knocked himself across the room, blowing a fuse. Another time he had frozen some crickets, still alive, then thawed them out. Nothing ever came back to life.

"Once they're dead, they're dead," he'd said. "The rest is fake."

But by the time she landed at La Guardia, Woody had revived. He grinned when she walked into the room. Clear tubes were hooked behind his ears in a jaunty way and ran into his nose. He looked like the ghost of Calvin, or the fetus, long and thin and pale. Calvin sat on the bed in workboots, jeans, and a tight T-shirt. Calvin and Woody used to call each other "she" and dress in tutus every Halloween. But lately Calvin had been working out, and he seemed to have grown muscles in his arms. Making a fist, he feinted with his left at Woody lying in the bed.

"This guy was just fooling us. This *clod*."

Woody feinted back. "That's *Sir* Clod to you, vassal. Yeah, it was just a ruse to get you here. You fell for it."

It was true, he didn't seem exactly sick, laughing in the bed. He told stories about his dance teacher, who thought he was a football coach.

"He grunts at us and tries to make us stomp. *Kill it, you wuss*, he says. *Kill it. Crush that step*."

He teased Calvin about some big, dumb saxophonist he was pining for. Gazing into Margy's eyes, he gave her hand a stroke.

"So how are you *really*?" he asked, exactly like Calvin.

Finally a nurse asked them to leave. "He needs to sleep."

"Yeah," said Woody. "You guys are putting me to sleep. Go to Max's party, for God's sake. Tell him I'll be there next time."

Calvin stood up. "You wish. He's not inviting you, you churl. And I'm *not* saying hello to anyone in a lip-ring."

They took a cab back to the Village, almost giddy as the lights flashed by.

"Doctors!" Calvin said, laughing. "I know a guy whose doctor said he had three months to live, and now he runs the New York Marathon. But his doctor, hey! He dropped dead of a heart attack. What makes them think they're such seers?"

"Hey, maybe you should get some sleep," she said. He seemed a little hollow-eyed.

"No way. Not now. And everyone'll be so glad to hear that Woody's fine."

At Woody's cramped apartment, she called Webster to say everything was fine. His machine picked up, though it was dark there by this time. She hung up quietly. In the morning, back from Dana's bed, he'd hear a click and nothing more. Well, that was fine. After bathing, she put on a silver sweater that emphasized her breasts, tight pants and high heels, and fluffed her hair up high.

The party was at Calvin's former teacher's, up on Riverside. Max had been a famous cellist once, and he still taught ("but only *handsome* students," Calvin said). His elegant apartment had a view of yellow lights on black water, and it was packed, with everyone from Leonard Bernstein down to Max's teenaged protégés. The party had already reached the dancing stage. Music agitated every particle of air. Everyone shouted in someone's ear. Margy danced with Calvin, then with two guys from Juilliard, cellists who worked with Max but clearly were not gay, glancing at her breasts and looking guiltily away. She'd felt self-conscious all her life, dancing where anyone could see. But what did she care now? She was the most relaxed she'd ever been. Swilling wine, she danced the way Dana walked *(men want me).*

Calvin gripped her shoulders, yelled, "You're radiating sex. What have you been doing out there in the great Wild West?"

She laughed, tossed back her head, and turned to see a young violinist she had once taught for a few months. Jean-Marc was Alsatian, ringleted, nineteen at most, and the summer she had taught him, he'd followed her around, gazing at her with sad eyes while she told him not to muscle Mozart to his will. Now he cut her out from the two cellists like a collie herding sheep.

"What are you *doing* here?" he cried. He kissed her on both cheeks and clutched her arms, though they'd never touched before. "You've come to drive me crazy, is that so?"

They danced, and Jean-Marc kept his hands on her, pushing the hair out of her eyes. After a while, it seemed the friendly thing to let him press his smooth, young tongue into her mouth. He felt fresh and boyish, packed with coiled erotic springs.

"I never wanted you to be my teacher," he groaned and pressed his hands all over her, as if trying to collapse her small enough to fold.

How dull her life seemed usually! All those sexless years, waiting. Why shouldn't she have lovers everywhere, like Webster or Michael? It was a way to feel no pain. Make a palimpsest of one lover on another and you didn't feel a thing, except well-being, like some pink magnolia flinging petals wide. She'd have to thank Webster for showing her.

～

"SHIT," Calvin yelled. "FUCKING SHIT."

It was still night, and he knelt on the stone abutment of a bridge she didn't recognize, leaning out above black water. Only a few cars roared by, the bridge deserted in the hot, soggy dark, and she was fairly certain they should not be there. She almost hadn't caught him, sandals sliding on damp sidewalks, as he ran across deserted roadways, up stairs reeking of piss. When they came back from the party, there had been a message from the hospital telling Calvin to return. It took a while to find a cab, and when they rushed up to Woody's room, the bed was bare. He had been moved down to the morgue. Above the East River, she got her arms around Calvin's waist as it bellowed in and out.

"FUCK. FUCK THIS SHIT."

She just held on. There was nothing else to do. It seemed possible that Calvin could die too, the bridge could collapse, time could stop. She kept her arms around him so hard for so long, she couldn't feel them when he pried them off. He wasn't crying. He was dignified and seemed to float in calm, his eyes remote and dry. As they walked back to the hospital, the world had ended, and the sky was getting light. She clutched Calvin's sleeve, and then his wrist, gilded with blond hair. But he did not take her hand.

~

California looked like Tuscany with no Florence. Empty hills in vapid yellow light, crawling with rattlesnakes. Poison oak stood ten feet high disguised in morning-glory vines. Roses frothed up pink and red on thorns that never died.

She'd only come to get her things and say good-bye. This time, she would not shout. Spit would not fly from her mouth. She would get on a plane. Calvin would be in Chicago, and they'd have to deal with new music, the fall season on the way.

"Call me the second you get in," said Webster's tenor on her aunt's machine. She listened to it twice. It felt like shards of glass exploded in her crotch. *Erase*, she pushed. Walking to the closet, she pulled out suitcases and began to pack.

Suddenly the door downstairs burst open, and Webster bounded up, looking like a genie let out of a bottle, gleeful and at large. He swept her up, pressed her full length to him, kissed her neck.

"Why didn't you call me? I would have come to meet you." His head turned toward the closet. "What's this?" He let her slide down toward the floor. "I see. Were you even going to tell me?"

Walking into the bathroom, she turned on the tap.

"Of course I was. I just got here. I haven't even had a bath, and you know how it feels, all day on planes. I'm covered with transcontinental grit."

She waited while the tub filled, but he didn't answer her. Turning off the tap, she called in a cheerful voice.

"You know I have to get back now. My aunt will be home soon."

Pulling off her linen pants, she tested the water, so hot it alarmed her skin as if with cold.

"Don't go yet," he said behind her. "You could stay in the boathouse when your aunt gets here. Or we could go somewhere."

"That might be nice, of course. But then, I have this job, two thousand miles from here. I have to get back."

He leaned against the sink and twirled a button on his blue workshirt, clean and freshly ironed. Since when did he wear ironed shirts? She'd never noticed any irons around his place. Did someone do it for him, somewhere else? Sinking into the water, she let it cover her mouth.

"One of us could move," he said slowly, looking down. "Get a job in the other's place."

Something pounced in Margy's chest. She lifted her mouth above the waterline.

"That might be something to consider, when we stop seeing other people."

His face came into sudden focus. He stared at her. "Seeing other people? I'm not seeing other people. Are you?"

Really, it was too hot in the tub. Turning on the cold, she swished the water with both hands like a six-year-old.

"Why, sure. Since you told me you were seeing Dana. It's all right, I knew it from the start. It's understood."

Keeping both hands behind him on the sink, he seemed braced against a blast. "You slept with someone else. In New York."

She hadn't quite gotten into bed with Jean-Marc, no. But now she wanted Webster to think so. Feeling rather naked, she picked up a washcloth and draped it across her breasts.

"While you were here, doing the same thing. With Dana."

He sprang from the sink, trembling like a tuning fork. "Jesus *Christ*. What kind of life have you had?"

In seconds he was down the stairs and out. The slam quivered the walls. The water in the tub rippled, and gradually went still. She wasn't wrong, was she? Of course she wasn't wrong. It was too much. A stupid sob leaped up her throat and stopped.

Downstairs, the door reopened, and the floor groaned with his heavy tread. In seconds, his eyes loomed over her, too large and black, alert, his breath controlled.

"Listen. Words are treacherous. When I say I'm seeing Dana, I don't mean I'm fucking her. Sometimes we go out to eat, or we take a walk. That's it. Nothing else."

She shrank down in the tub. "And she cries and tries to get you into bed, and you won't go?"

He winced. "Something like that."

He stared at the wall above her head. "It wasn't Calvin? Someone new. You slept with someone new in New York."

She went hard, deflecting this. If he hadn't slept with Dana, what about the rest of them? There had been others, she was sure of it.

Kneeling on the tile, he took hold of her shoulders, his face six inches from hers.

"You're not very observant, you realize that? You think you know what's happening, but you miss a lot. Like the fact that I'm in love with you. I want to marry you. Come out of there," he said and lifted her up, stunned and dripping, from the tub.

～

It was a hot, dry afternoon in a courtroom usually reserved for small claims and misdemeanors. At the last minute, Calvin had turned up, in the car of a San Francisco friend. He didn't smile, but he had brought a bag of pink rose petals, and he strewed them on the pale blue carpeting. Webster wore his mallard tie, Margy a linen suit she'd bought three days before, one size too large and altered awkwardly. A good blue suit, her mother had always said, was the only proper thing if you were not a virgin, or divorced, all wrong brides.

She'd gotten through the last few days mostly asleep, face smashed into Webster's chest, as if she'd landed there from a great height. In the intervals of wakefulness, she wondered, could you marry someone you had known only two months?

"When you meet the person you are going to marry, you don't question it," Webster had said. With eerie calm, he had made plans to move to Chicago. Lake Michigan had plankton, even jellyfish. He swore it would be only a small change for him.

Now she felt ghostly, passion-free, translucent, possibly, as she stepped up to the bleakly modern rail, holding Webster's hand in front of God and the county treasurer. The treasurer was a woman in a Balinese-print suit, ivory elephants on twisted strands around her neck. She opened a wide book, mispronouncing Webster's name.

"Love is like the rain," she said. "Patient and forgiving, falling on parched ground. Love makes it spring year-round."

"Elephants died to make your necklace," Webster said, shaking her official hand.

Then they were outside, in a mammoth parking lot beside a six-lane freeway ringed with parched gold slopes the size of small mountains. The building was designed by Frank Lloyd Wright to imitate the hills and sky, but painted wrong, pink and royal blue like a Mexican funeral home. Calvin tried to get it in the pictures, standing too far back while Margy and Webster squinted in the sun. Calvin had lost weight, and in the bright sun he appeared thin-skinned, blue under the eyes. A year before, he might have worn pink tulle, or three ties from flea markets. But now he still had on the same black suit and white T-shirt he had worn at Woody's funeral.

"Will you be all right?" she asked and clung to him, realizing suddenly that she would get into the car with Webster, and Calvin would not. They had a room reserved on the north coast and had to leave to make it there by dark.

Calvin snorted. "You're the one who's just gone racing full speed off a cliff, and you're asking me if I'll be all right?"

Webster shook his hand, and Calvin seemed to look at him for the first time.

"Nice tie," he said.

Webster loosened it, pulled it off over his head, and held it out like a noose. Calvin looked surprised, ready to refuse.

"Groom's gift," Webster said. "For the best man, you know."

Calvin's chin rose.

"I was the *maid* of honor," he said, dignified. But he slipped the tie over his head and hung it loose on his bare neck. As they drove away, he scattered rose petals over the hood.

"Wait," Margy gasped.

But wait for what? If they were going, they would have to go. Webster stopped the car.

"You did everything you could to get away from me, and it didn't work. So you might as well relax."

But Margy knew that this was no time to relax. From now on, she would stay alert and notice everything. Nothing would escape her. Sunlight slanted through the windshield, and rose petals shifted on the hood. When the car moved, they flew up, pressed against the glass like small pink tongues, then blew away.

When a Miwok Takes a Wife

~~~~~~~~~~~~~~~

He used to float his kayak underneath her house and cling to pilings like a barnacle. He listened for her feet, bare skin on wood or little loafers soft as moccasins. He couldn't think. He couldn't breathe. The first note of the violin gave him a rush of endocrines so strong he had to put his head between his knees. She liked to play a little sweet-sad melody in minor key, and it was a huge sound, monstrously alive. It took hold of him, stroked under his skin, places he couldn't reach. He felt swollen like a bruise, ready to split open, bleed.

"I'm sorry," was the first thing she ever said to him.

"Sorry for what?" he wanted to shout. Something about the violin, as if it bothered him. Her eyes bulged green behind thick wire-frames, warped like fish in an aquarium. She gave him the most alive look he had ever seen, curious, half laughing, afraid.

Now she was his, and he could take her clothes off any time he liked. She had the smoothest skin he'd ever felt, creamy as a fat woman's, though she was small and fine. It didn't make a difference how many times he heaved himself at her like a salmon up a waterfall. Parts of him ached on unsatisfied, arms to pull her up against his chest, fingers for her skin. His nose needed to press against her bones, flattening the tip. It was a need he hadn't known a nose could have. He'd been drawn to women's flesh since he was nine or ten, never before to women's bones.

"What's the Algonquian for 'wife'?" she asked as they walked along Bolinas Beach. He didn't know. *Ouiouin* was to marry, *napema* a married man. But the baron's dictionary gave no word for married women, as if they didn't count, or didn't count to the baron. The Miwok might have had one, right here on this beach, but there was no way to find out. A chill ran over him. The wind was picking up, and Margy's hair waved free like tentacles.

"Let's go home." Hooking an arm around her neck, he pressed his nose into the hard bone of her head.

She helped him pack his field notes and his books. He sold the kayak, after one last paddle past the reef. He was eager to leave Bolinas now. The place was full of sad and solitary guys, lonely walkers in the fog, of whom he was no doubt considered one. But his research was all done. He'd write the dissertation in Chicago, and when he had the doctorate, he would become the ocean man in some lake lab. The Great Lakes were like oceans, but more fragile, closed, and the declines he charted would be even more clear. As Margy said, at least in Chicago you knew you weren't killing anything.

They drove across the country in an old yellow Mercedes that had been her father's once. It had ripped leather seats and hints of rust around the rims, but it was so wide and solid, one day they pulled off the road and made love in the back seat, by a sunny pasture, giggling. That was Nebraska, where the sky was high and Western, washed-out blue. The air began to thicken after that. The sky sank lower, gray and wet, until it hung right over them.

Hours before he thought they had arrived, Chicago came out to meet them. Seven million people behind brick and glass, several thousand square miles of brown buildings hunched three stories tall. Buckled, potholed streets, with bombed-out factories and rusted iron and broken concrete and exploded glass heaped up in empty lots. Plastic grocery sacks blew past. In every block three dumpsters bulged up to capacity. Yellow steam trailed to the ground, scented of steel mills, bus exhaust.

Margy's apartment looked over the lake, green and shimmering to the horizon on three sides. But her apartment was a box, not much bigger than the boathouse and six floors off the ground. She followed him from room to room, watching with startled eyes, as if she had not imagined how he'd look inside the place. She brushed against him, gentle as a cat, and pleasure radiated out from where she touched.

"I need to practice," she said, note of panic in her voice.

"Can I listen?"

Her eyes went wild. "No one ever listens to me practicing."

"I did for months."

She set her music stand up in the living room, facing the lake, and he retreated to the bedroom with a book. She tuned up, thrashed out some frenetic bars, and stopped. Standing at the bedroom door, she held the bow and violin.

"I'm too aware of you, but I need to get used to it. Maybe you could come in here?"

He stood behind her while she played, watching her body merge into the instrument. Her hair was pinned up, flattened to her head to keep it off the strings, and her neck looked much too small to stand the way it clutched the violin. He moved in, brushed his lips across the fine gold down, the lit-

ANTCR

tle vertebrae shifting. She shivered. Goosebumps prickled on her skin. Craning her head around, she looked at him.

"Play that again," he said into her ear and stroked her breasts. She leaned against him, played the sweet-sad melody that used to torture him. How much better was this now!

~

She started to rehearse for the fall season, and he made a home for them. He found a store that had organic vegetables and meat, shampoo in bulk, no need to buy plastic. The city of Chicago had no recycling, but he drove their glass and metal up to Evanston. He found a midwife who could teach them natural birth control, requiring no poisons, no trash, no plastic wrap, except for a few days each month. They learned the signs her body made, as it prepared to be unsafe, and tracked them on a chart.

"It's a little drama every month," she said. "The music starts, the curtain parts, and then, voila, the egg!"

She got him a ticket to her first concert, in a high balcony. He watched her through his field glasses, her hair the only spot of yellow in a sea of black, her arm pumping in time with all the rest. But they had to pay for him, and it was fabulously expensive. So most nights he stayed home and played her records or the radio. After a while he thought he could tell Bach from Brahms, Schoenberg from Stravinsky, Mozart from everyone. He tried to find the little sweet-sad tune Margy played, and never heard it anywhere.

"It's nothing," Margy said.

"What is it? Don't you know?"

"I'm not sure. My head's too full of music. I must have heard it somewhere."

"I bet you made it up."

"I doubt it. I've never made up anything." But she looked pleased, secretly.

When she was finished for the night, they drank a glass of wine and talked about her day. Once it was a guest conductor who berated them all afternoon, made them play the same phrase fifty-seven times. Then he beamed at them all through the show as if they'd done it perfectly, when it sounded just the same. Another time it was a soprano who used a French accent, pretended not to know some ordinary English words, though she was from Detroit.

"*Complètement fou.* How do you say?" She'd wave a hand, giving a Gallic shrug. She wanted everyone to think she had a glamorous background, when she was Motown all the way.

Margy overheard a hapless journalist ask her what instrument she played.

"I'm *Linda Gaudreau*," she said, as if to crush him with her name.

Webster filled the tub for Margy, rubbed her shoulders till she could relax. He dried her off and carried her to bed, stroked her to sleep. Mornings he woke her up with orange juice and tea, coaxed her to stay a while before she started practicing. But finally he had to let her go, to do it all again.

~~

He made a lab table out of a door and squeezed it into the dining room. He taped his field notes on *Aurelia* around the walls. The last year in Bolinas, he had noticed something odd about the jellyfish. He could always find their early plankton forms along the reef, the ones that looked like many-legged worms or plantlike polyps rooted to a rock. But no matter how often he searched, he rarely found the final two stages. They had to break free first as swimming stars, to reach the final transformation, when they grew legs and bent them back, turned inside out to form the bell-shaped bodies they would keep. Only then did they gain sex, grow up to spawn.

Why were they stalling out instead as eunuch polyps? It could be a form of birth control. Animals knew when to keep their numbers down, as did the Indians. A Miwok woman with two children gave up any other to be killed at birth, the father stomping on its neck, so there would always be enough army worms to go around. But jellyfish were not just in decline. They'd disappeared beyond a certain stage, less like birth control than mass suicide.

He analyzed the water on the reef for every kind of chemical, but it was cleaner than it had been in the 1970s. It was also a bit warmer, but less than a degree, and state-funded scientists made light of the change at conferences. *Aurelia aurita* lived in every ocean, including the China Sea and Gulf of Mexico, where water temperatures could rise to 85 degrees. It could adapt to live at nine degrees below its lethal limit. Near Bolinas, on the other hand, the water felt like ice, a frigid 59 even in summertime. So why should tiny rises make a difference?

One day in the airless Berkeley library, he found an obscure study on the plankton jellyfish of north Scotland. The ocean there was almost arctic, and jellyfish lived happily. Except, the Scottish researcher noticed, even the smallest rise in temperature seemed to stall them at the polyp stage, especially when food supplies were down. Webster's first published article had shown that plankton shrimp were in decline off the California coast. And plankton shrimp happened to be the favorite food of baby jellyfish.

His adviser let him set up tanks to demonstrate the theory in his Berkeley lab, with sterile sea water he made himself. Webster captured baby jellyfish to live in them and plankton shrimp for them to eat, but just enough to duplicate their food supplies out in the ocean now. Three tanks he kept as cold as the ocean in a normal year, three warmer by one-half degree. After a month, the cold tanks swarmed with floating stars and miniature medusas, not quite big enough to see. But in the warm tanks, polyps drooped their tentacles, began to die.

So it was clear then, wasn't it? And all he had to do was write up the results. Perched at his lab table in Margy's dining room, index fingers poised above his manual typewriter, he wondered where to start. "Global warming," "geothermal disaster," "ethical insanity"?

He typed the first few lines.

"Hey!" Margy called from where she stood playing the violin, about ten feet away. "Could you maybe do that in six-eight time?"

He moved to the wobbly kitchen table, but it wasn't far enough away. The violin seemed suddenly too loud, like arrows on his skin. He took the typewriter into the bathroom, closed the door, and hunched on the cold tile floor. All his length contorted in a fold, like a cicada trying to molt, he stared up through the only window at the sky. Sometimes a cloud went by, sometimes a gull.

～

After a month, he'd tapped out all he could, though the result was shorter than he'd hoped. He made up a few charts and graphs, put all the numbers in, threw in a sermon at the end. The case he'd made was strong. He didn't need to pad it out. One warm fall day, he packed the pages up and mailed them off to his adviser in Berkeley.

Waiting for the reply, he bought books on lakes, full of the digestive tracks of worms. Mornings, while Margy practiced, he took his run, dipped sample jars along the lake. So far, when he checked them in the microscope, he found almost nothing in them wiggling. But even in the fall there should be plankton, and he started swimming out into the warm green lake to look for them. He swam a quarter mile, then a half mile from shore, before he took the cap off the sample jar. Any day now he might find what he was looking for, *Crustacea*, *Gastropoda*, *Scyphozoa* glimmering beneath the scope.

"I had the strangest dream," Margy said one morning in the kitchen as he was getting ready to set off. "We were in Bolinas, making love, and my aunt came in. When she left, we tried again, but your penis was detached. I tried to put it in myself, but it was wobbly as a worm. I held it up and said, 'You ought to keep this attached to yourself!'"

"Jesus," Webster said. He had a large erection suddenly, so big it seemed to pull the skin tight on his whole body.

Margy laughed, reached for his shorts. "That's some reaction to castration. Or was it because I wanted to put even your detached penis inside of me?"

Webster couldn't say, didn't care. He just wanted to go back to bed. It was a Sunday, and she went with him. They spent the whole morning in bed, then strolled out, leaning on each other, ate sushi for lunch. They took a cab to the aquarium. Everywhere they went, she whipped out credit cards or twenty-dollar bills to pay, while Webster watched uneasily.

"You'll take a year off when I have a job," he murmured in her ear as they stared at long-nosed tropical turtles. Margy beamed up at him, green eyes shining.

"I don't need a year off. That is, unless we have a baby."

Webster kissed her head. The need for babies seemed somewhat diminished, here in the aquarium, where everyone had two or three in strollers, toddling off to heave their juice bottles into the alligator pen. Meanwhile, the California otters had to swim around a tank about the size of a Volkswagen van. Paddling on their backs, they circled rapidly, knowing where the corners were.

"What?" they seemed to say, turning furry faces toward the crowd behind the glass. "What do you want?"

~~

Webster lay awake for several nights, imagining how he could liberate the sea otters. He'd get a job at the aquarium, try to become the otters' keeper and possess the keys. He'd put them in a crate and drive them to the airport, forge the health certificates, and take them on a plane. Once in San Francisco, he would drive them down to Monterey and watch them swim away. But could he keep the otters happy through the move? There might be guards at the aquarium, even in the middle of the night. He saw himself with the three otters in a golf bag, terrified and squealing, the cops stopping him. The cops would not know how to take care of the otters. It might hurt them in the end. Should he work through legal channels instead, and start a movement, bumper stickers, billboards on the street? It would take funds, a catchy slogan. "Otters Oughter Have a Bigger Pen"?

Haggard from lack of sleep, he started to include the aquarium on his daily run. He ran around it, looked at all the doors. It was a little nuts, but he couldn't help himself. He was starting to suspect that this was not a healthy place for otters or for anyone. Past the aquarium, a point projected out into the lake, and he swam out from it to dip his sample jars. But when he checked them through the scope, nothing was in them, nothing, not a living thing.

One day, as he came back from his run and swim, the mailman was just slouching up their block, a big blond Pole who left the smell of cigar smoke even inside the envelopes. He was a fan of Margy's, and he liked to give her his opinion of the last thing she had played. ("That Mahler was a little over-Bached," he'd say around his cigar. "Mahler should be mushy, not precise.") Sometimes he brought no mail for weeks, then piles of it, well smoked.

"Nice as California!" he called and grinned, exhaling smoke. And it was true, it was a clear fall day, if you ignored the smells of sulfur and roof tar.

The man had dropped a package off, and he recognized

the envelope, rumpled, crossed out, readdressed. His dissertation, returned. His adviser must have things he wanted fixed. He ripped the flap off as he climbed the stairs, dripping. It smelled exactly like cigar.

Inside, with the pages he had typed, was an article just out in an important journal, citing Webster's shrimp work as "the kind of simple-minded environmentalism rampant in the field today," this part highlighted in yellow to make sure he saw it. Shrimp populations varied according to their own laws, the author said, and global warming, pesticides, and fertilizers played no part. At the end of the article, after the author's name, was the name of a major West Coast power company.

"I thought you might get away with it," his adviser's letter said. "But it looks like not. This time you'll have to rub their noses in it. Do the chemistry on the beasts themselves and prove that it's the temperature and nothing else. Then see what they have to say."

Webster read the letter twice, slower the second time. To show chemical changes in the jellyfish, he'd have to murder millions of them in the lab machines, become the Butcher of Bolinas, a one-man jellyfish blight. His adviser was a grizzled, bearded Englishman with jowls who wore the same tan corduroys week after week and had once done major work on early eye-bud development in crabs, which had required the sacrifice of several thousand animals. Webster avoided killing anything. He liked to nurse the jellyfish until they were just big enough to see, each one a small disturbance on the surface of the water, then ferry them out to the reef and watch them pulse away. Was he supposed to net the same ones now and crush them into little piles of sodium and ash?

He wrote a letter to his adviser: "Jellyfish numbers are already down. Doing the chemistry would be like euthanizing Bengal tigers to find out why hunters slaughter them. You know I'm right. The population studies are enough. I'll do more research, but not if it means hurting jellyfish."

"How important is this to you, Hale?" his adviser wrote back, though he knew that was no longer Webster's name. "It isn't going to pop together just because you need it to, now that you've left the area. I'm afraid I will have to insist, if you want me involved in this."

"Couldn't you go out there for a while?" Margy asked that night as they washed dishes. "Do the research, get it over with? How long could it take?"

He held a plate up, rinsed it with a quick burst from the tap. Margy preferred the dishwasher, but he had showed her that it wasn't necessary for two plates. It could be done with just a pint of water, conserving everything.

"It's not a question of time." He held the plate up, let the drops fall back into the pan. Margy took it, dried.

"But you'd be finished then. You could get a job." Carefully she polished it, examining the finish on the plate.

～

He went back to his typewriter and wrote a new letter, to a professor who had once admired his work. The dissertation was all written and enclosed and all he needed was a signature. Would the professor consider taking over as his adviser at this stage? He mailed the dissertation off again.

This time while he waited, he gave the apartment a real cleaning. He scrubbed the ceilings, under the refrigerator, back behind the stove, and was appalled at what he found. Old lipstick tubes, lost bow rosin, petrified potatoes from five years ago. How could Margy live like this? She never cleaned. She never even straightened anything. Any room where she had been would have a trail across it, damage of some kind. Pages ripped out of a book or scrawled with ink. She took one bite out of an apple, left the rest to rot. One day he counted six abandoned pairs of shoes from room to room.

He could hear her in the next room, talking on the phone.

"He's full of shit, but he's adorable," she said. Webster paused, listening. *Who's full of shit?*

But she just laughed, hung up. When he went into the living room, she was studying a sheaf of music, Tobias Picker, "Invisible Lilacs."

"You know, for the two of us to live in this small space, we need to keep it straight," he said gently.

She tipped her head back, and her eyes swam with amusement behind the thick lenses.

"Why, it's the archangel and his flaming sword. Out, shoes! Out, dust! Go wander the world!"

"Very funny. But you see what I mean? There won't be room to breathe in here by spring."

Half an hour later, she had not touched the shoes, and it was time for her to leave. Whirling through the apartment, she left swaths of wadded tissue, tennis shoes, damp towels.

"Can't talk. See you later. Bye." She blew him kisses, slammed the door. Seconds later she swept back in to grab the music she had left, swept out again.

Webster cleaned up, put the shoes away. Walking to the store, he bought organic vegetables for soup, took his run and cleaned. He spent the evening reading about lamprey blight, while he simmered potato peels for broth. He knew what time she would be finished, how long it would take for her to change out of her concert clothes, get to the car, drive home. He chopped celery and onions, sautéed them in olive oil, simmered potatoes in the broth, saving tomatoes, broccoli, and herbs for last. The soup was perfect at the moment when she should walk in.

The phone rang instead.

"I've got to go to this reception. Sorry, I should have mentioned it. This big swell who funds the symphony. I can't get out of it. Don't worry. Calvin will take me."

Webster didn't mind Calvin, the only man alive besides himself who'd ever treated Margy well. True, she was awfully close to Calvin, told him everything and even wore his clothes. It helped that he was gay, and lived in their building, two floors down, so she could ride with him to the symphony at night. At least with Calvin she'd be safe.

"How late will you be?"

"I don't know. Midnight at most. Don't worry."

But she wasn't home at midnight, and he put the soup away before he fell asleep. Some time that night, he felt her slide between the sheets, smelling of cigar.

"You smell like the mail," he murmured and seized her. Who had she been with who had smoked cigars? The spike of jealousy went straight to wanting her.

She inched away. "Sorry, I'm too beat. Go back to sleep."

But he couldn't stop. Who knew where she had been? He insisted, and she went along, limply. Afterward she fell into a heavy sleep, chin pointed toward the ceiling, lips ajar. Long breaths rattled like waves through gravel, going out.

He woke before she did and wanted her again. All his protoplasm streamed toward her. Alarmed, she leaped up, filled the tub.

"I have to take a bath."

He followed, stroking her. "Come back to bed."

"Can't. Got to practice. I have no idea what to do with this thing we're supposed to play today."

Quickly she explained about the piece, some brand-new symphony that called for police whistles and bike bells and fog horns. It made demands on violinists she had never seen before. Bathing fast, she rushed out to the living room and started squeezing tortured sounds out of the violin.

She had four shows that week and stayed out late after each one. Receptions, galas, fund-raisers, she said. Webster

waited up and sniffed her over carefully. She smelled like cigarettes, champagne, blue cheese, sushi, strange perfumes, and
concert sweat. One night she smelled like burnt sugar and
said it was a dessert soaked in brandy, set on fire. None of it
put him off. The pressure built up as he waited hours for her,
wondered where she was. He couldn't help it. He extracted
tolls from her, every night and in the morning too.

"Twice a day is too much," she gasped finally one morning
as she shrank away.

He could barely speak, he wanted her so much.

"It wasn't last summer."

"I was on vacation then. Now I have other things to do.
I'm exhausted all the time."

"You wouldn't be if you came home at night."

He whimpered, stroking her. She gave in, stayed in bed
with him.

On Sunday night that week she had agreed to play a benefit for Haitian refugees, and afterward she called to say there
was a party and she'd better go.

"No," Webster said, the word out of his mouth before he
noticed it. *Come home and take a bath with me,* was what he
meant, but he couldn't organize his tongue.

There was a silence on the phone.

"No?" Her laugh came light and musical. "Is that really what you said? Look, you know you could come down and go with us. I'll get you a tux, and you can come along and help to chat up donors any time you like. How does that sound?"

She knew he'd planned his life to avoid such events. Even for their wedding he had made it clear there'd be no family, no guests, and no reception line. So now all he could do was demand when she would be home, though she'd ignore it if she wanted to.

At midnight, he shoved a window up and watched the cars six floors below. Pacing between the window and the stairs, he kept an eye on Calvin's door. He couldn't read. He was too anxious to sit down. How did he get into this state? He'd lived alone for years, liked it. What was happening to him?

He lay on the couch and didn't know he was asleep until he woke up with a start. It was after two, and Margy wasn't home. Leaning out into the cool night air, he checked the block but couldn't see the old Mercedes anywhere.

After a while, it drove up, idled in the street. There were no spaces left, but Margy wedged it in by a hydrant, where the ticket would be worth a week of groceries. He heard her laugh as she and Calvin stepped out of the car.

Suddenly, he didn't want to talk to her. Switching off the lights, he shed his clothes and slid under the comforter, lay like a dead man.

She tiptoed past him, closed the bathroom door. Humming on the other side, she filled the tub. Her buttons clicked on the tile floor. Soap smells drifted out with whiffs of steam and water rippling. He was almost actually asleep when she slid in next to him and ran her tongue along his spine. His body woke up all the way at once, but he resisted it.

"What?" she whispered, lips against his ear from behind. "What do you want? Isn't this it?"

Not only this, he could have said, but then she might have stopped. Sighing, he rolled over, took her wrists. His fingers overlapped, encircled them. Small bones, flexible. He could have snapped them with one flick, but what would that get him? Her breath came quick against his neck. When she tried to pull away and look at him, he clamped his cheek against her ear and held it there, safe from her eyes.

～

His dissertation came back from the new professor he had sent it to. The man said he would like to help, but he had talked to Webster's old adviser, and they had discussed it with the whole group in marine biology. The group decided Webster should come back to Berkeley and do more research. If he didn't, they agreed there was no way they could grant him a degree.

Climbing the stairs from the mailbox, Webster considered flying out to burn down the biology building. As he walked into the apartment, it looked different to him. His field notes on *Aurelia* were still attached to every wall. What was he thinking, leaving them up everywhere? Yank, he ripped them down along the hall. Yank, yank, yank, he reached the dining room.

It was a Saturday, and Margy had a rare day off. In the kitchen, she made salad, humming. Reaching for a page of notes, he saw her tear a paper towel off the roll. Fascinated, he watched while she dried one lettuce leaf and tossed the towel into the trash. She did it twice, three times. When she reached for a fourth, he raced into the kitchen, and his hand shot out to stop the roll.

"Paper towels are trees. At least use it again. Or this," he said and offered her a linen towel, one of ten some friend of hers had given them when they got married, just three full moons ago.

She flinched. "You dry your hands on that, and you expect me to use it on something we're going to eat?"

He glanced at his hands involuntarily. "Do you think everything you eat is sterilized? There are about a million germs inside your mouth right now. Not to mention on your skin, your eyelashes, under your nails . . . "

He didn't know where to begin. Creatures too small to see lived all over her, most of them not hurting anything. Mitochondria inside her cells, lactobacilli that helped digest her food. Three hundred million of his sperm thrashed happily inside her after every single time.

She shuddered, opened the refrigerator. "My, you think such lovely things. I've always wondered what goes on inside your head. Is it all just jellyfish and germs in people's mouths? Or do you ever think about the people you know, what they're like and what they say to you? And music, things like that?"

He had once been drawn to crab development, before he noticed shrimp. But he didn't feel like saying that. In fact, he didn't feel like saying anything. He watched her take a small container out and set it on the counter. He picked it up. *Pot au crème*, it said. *Crème fraiche*. How many times had he asked her not to buy plastic they'd have to throw away? For centuries, millennia, this little pot would stay intact, long after Margy herself rotted into compost, dried to dust, rejoined the atmosphere as a carbon cloud.

"Why did you buy this?"

She glanced up, focused on his hand. "What? Oh, for heaven's sake."

She tried to take the pot. A wave of fury blinded him. His fist convulsed, the cap popped up. A dome of white cream crested out like pus.

"What are you doing?" She snatched it away from him.

He stalked out of the room, feeling as if he might explode. Was it because he would not get a Ph.D. from Berkeley? No, it was Margy and the cream container. He felt insane.

"We'll use it again," she called from the kitchen cheerfully.

He wasn't listening. Putting on running shorts, he shoved his feet into moccasins and tied his hair back with a leather thong. He needed to get out of here. He had to think. Strapping a small blue nylon pack with sample jars around his naked waist, he burst out the front door and thundered down the stairs.

It was November now, but strangely warm, and half the city had turned out along the breakwater with bicycles and strollers, dogs and children, several thousand barbecues. The air was mainly charcoal smoke, flavored with lighter fluid, car exhaust, and sauerkraut from hot dog stands. Near Oak Street Beach, one man was barbecuing in his car. The metal dish lay on the floor of his front seat, and flames shot up around the dash, while the guy, a heavy, white-skinned blond about nineteen, clutched a baby to his naked chest and shoved the meat around.

Webster escaped onto the clanking metal bridge that crossed the river to the south and fought through strolling crowds again, never quite reaching his stride. At last he arrived at the aquarium, the planetarium, the landing strip for private planes. Asphalt shimmered in the heat, and he ran across it fast to reach the farthest dike. *No Swimming, No Diving*, a sign said on the chain-link fence. Beyond it, water glinted through the haze, green and pearl-pink where a swell shifted.

Three black men squatted by a cooler on the dike, near the only opening along the fence. One of them was tall and lean in cut-off jeans, and he stood up and glared as Webster approached. Webster didn't slow. As he passed them on the narrow cement strip, he gave a nod and loped to the far end.

Stepping from his moccasins, he unstrapped the pack and took a sample jar, dove in. Tepid, cooler underneath, the water smelled faintly of burning rubber and felt soapy as it slid across his skin.

He swam a few minutes and turned to see how far he'd gone. Treading, checking with his feet for dead cars, old refrig-

erators, bodies anchored in cement, he noticed that the tall
black man was running down the dike. He threw both arms
into the air, yelling something Webster couldn't quite make
out. He picked up Webster's pack and flung it out into the lake.

"Hey!" Webster yelled.

The moccasins went next. Suddenly the man was close
enough to hear. He roared.

"How'd you like me to fuck you in the ass?"

Webster paused only a moment, then swam back fast. The
moccasins were floating, but the pack was gone. There was no
question now of getting back onto the dike, with the guy leaping, foaming at the mouth. He had his shirt off, and his body
jerked, sweat flying off him. His eyes bulged red, his face contorted with the yelling mouth.

"How'd you like me to fuck you in the ass?"

Clutching his moccasins and one remaining sample jar, he
looked fast for another way to haul back out. The guy leaped
in and started swimming after him, still yelling as he swam.

"How'd you like me to fuck you in the ass?"

~

It was a long swim all the way around the point, and he ran
into an oil slick at the harbor mouth. But the guy fell back,

and Webster managed to haul out and run into the crowd without seeing him. He was acutely conscious of his bare skin, wet with lake water and oil and sweat. His knees shook. Did the guy think he was gay, or possibly female? People stared. He felt exposed, as if he had been shitting in public. Ashamed, he tried to run and almost couldn't move.

At last he got to their building, but didn't want to go up the front stairs, where he might see someone he knew. Unlocking the back gate, he quickly climbed the old, wood fire escape, trying to get out of sight.

A sound came down to meet him, caught him unaware. The violin, played huge. It was the goddamned sweet-sad tune. He had to sit down on the stairs and put his head between his knees. It took hold of him, stroked him where he couldn't reach. Swollen like a bruise, he waited to split open, bleed.

Flight

~~~~~~~~~~~~~~~~~~

One summer in Missouri woods, before the sun could boil the air, a small bird darted low from thick green vines, and, unable to stop, Webster's size-twelve running shoe came down on it. He was on the side of life. When he took plankton samples from farm ponds, he tried to let them go unhurt. Bugs lived undisturbed around his house. He tried not to eat meat. Dropping to his knees, he picked up the bird, a chickadee, delicate white windpipe popped through the chest wall like a rubber band. A minute before, it had flitted through the trees, loopy as a butterfly, calling cheerfully. Now it was limp, like a water balloon, only too small—more like a used condom. He felt an anxious flash. What was his wife doing, that minute, in Chicago?

It was an ancient, stupid thought, whispered by the sloth-brain at the bottom of his skull. There had been that bastard in New York, five years ago. She said she didn't fuck him, but who knew? Okay, they weren't married then, and now they were. Didn't that mean she wouldn't do it now? He put it from his mind and poked the windpipe back inside the chickadee, though it would never breathe again.

He had deaths already on his head. In school he had dissected frogs, later fetal pigs shot full of plastic goo, pink in their arteries and blue for veins, plus countless starfish, octopods, crustaceans, clams. He tried to stick to projects that had been designed to help some creature in decline. But the day always arrived when you had to cut the animal you were trying to save. He was now a grad student in lake biology, and to pay tuition, buy his books, he worked for a project on amphibians, why they laid fewer eggs the last few years, or eggs that didn't hatch, around the world. He wanted them to hatch, but every day he tried to make them stop, zapped frog eggs with fertilizer, pesticide, or ultraviolet rays. Brain surgeons learned to operate on cats. Dental students practiced cutting gums on live monkeys. You could specialize in the tiniest, most loathsome viruses and find yourself injecting them into baby bunnies to find out what they did.

He laid the chickadee on a tree limb, in case somehow it could wake up, and walked back to his campsite, in a glade by a sinkhole. He couldn't shake off the anxiety. The glade was full of black-eyed susans, bachelor buttons, and pink yarrow, and his Harley'd scored a trench through them. What had he accomplished, besides crushing flowers, birds? He'd been away from home almost a week, taken samples out of forty-seven ponds, most of them full of nitrates, PCBs, and chloridane, nothing that moved. The ponds were all just belly up, with X's on their eyes. There were another eighteen he should check. But what would happen if he went home instead and saw his wife?

He knew what Margy would be doing now. She'd be asleep, alone. The orchestra was playing in Ravinia, and soon she would get up to practice, standing in the living room, barefoot in shorts if it was warm. She might play nothing but one phrase a hundred times. When he was home, he liked to loiter near her, watch the muscles twitch in her thin arms, fingers oscillating on the strings like hummingbird wings. Sometimes he stood behind her, pressed against her while she played, let the music vibrate in his bones. It was almost as good as sex, depending on the piece (alas, it was all true, "Bolero" was the best). He followed her through the apartment, anxious if she went into the bathroom and closed the door. Was she all right in there? She wasn't making any noise.

Once when she had ordinary flu, she fainted while talking on the phone. She had been sitting sideways on a chair, and when she fell back, her head bounced half an inch above the floor. At night she had bad dreams. Sometimes she sat up and gave a rasping shriek as if her tongue had been removed: "Unnnnnnh! Unnnnnnnh!"

It was a big tube coming in the window, she would say, or a crevasse that opened underneath the bed. Once when he woke up, she was leaning out the window, six floors off the ground.

"We have to!" she yelped when he grabbed her.

"We have to what?"

Lights came on in her eyes. She couldn't remember.

She went to see a shrink, spent expensive hours discussing it. The shrink did not suggest she take a long vacation from the symphony. The shrink wanted to talk about Webster. Margy came home looking thoughtful.

"Did your parents abuse you?" she asked him casually. And, "Oh, by the way, when are you going to finish your degree, so we can have a child?"

Webster had almost finished his degree. He had in fact done two doctorates, the one at Berkeley and the one in Chicago on lakes, though he had not quite been awarded either. Nine years was perhaps too long to be a grad student, especially in science. But when he got things worked out in the lab, designed the right computer model for his work, refined the data, who knew what might happen? He could get both of them!

But that didn't mean he knew what their next step would be. Margy claimed he had said yes to children in the murky past, on the Pacific coast, where you could walk for miles and not see others of your kind. In Chicago, though, they lived with millions of their kind in the space of a small atoll, surrounded by each other's trash. He checked water drops that ought to teem with plankton and found them quite free of life. Was it really, logically, a human baby that was needed here?

He tried to joke. "Maybe when you get me out of Chicago."

She didn't laugh. "Sometimes I wonder if you could have filed your dissertation a long time ago."

"If only that were true," he said, and happily explained how freshwater plankton differed from their ocean counterparts, in ways that affected their population variance. She listened, sticking out her lower lip. Her face began to look like a small bulldozer.

"And that's the only reason? You really haven't finished it?"

Often she'd explained to him the right age for a woman to have her first baby (twenty-four), and pointed out how far she had exceeded it (nine years). She never mentioned her abortion, fifteen years ago. But the big tube in her dreams cut like a knife and tried to suck her up. The shrink was probably quite interested. But did that really, logically, have anything to do with him?

"You know what I've noticed lately?" she said. "You don't even kiss me like you mean it."

Webster stopped midstep. He had been on his way back to a chapter on the reproductive habits of freshwater snails.

"Like I mean it? Of course I mean it. What are you talking about?"

"Did you ever see that old commercial on TV, when we were kids? Bucky Beaver for Ipana, how it coats your teeth with this—knock, knock—invisible shield?" Making a fist, she knocked the air beside his chest. "It's like you've got this— knock, knock—invisible shield."

Webster smiled. "In bed, you mean. It's like I'm under glass in bed."

She gave a breathless shrug. "Sort of."

That night, he couldn't sleep, read late, and she had been asleep for hours when he finally slid between the sheets. She sat up in the dark.

"Unnnnnnh! Unnnnnnnh!" she shrieked, rasping.

He woke her up. "It's me. What did you think?"

"It was a hell-dog with huge dripping jaws. A hell-dog getting into bed with me!"

~

In his camp by the sinkhole, he packed his gear onto the bike and rolled out of the glade, trying to stay in the same rut he had already made. Driving dirt tracks, country roads, and freeways, skin encased in grime, sweat, motor oil, he reached the south end of Lake Michigan, where clouds of black smoke huffed from steel mills, and flames flickered in the gloom, while miles of pipe snaked over ground that could ignite if someone threw a match. The National Sacrifice Zone, as the EPA called it, meaning they could not protect this place at all. It included Chicago, where the only wildlife was the many million rats that lived on dog feces. Beside it all, green and tantalizing to the sky, gleamed the dead lake. On the Southside, his tires thumped over potholes like heartbeats. Passing the Loop, the near Northside, he turned off at Lincoln Park, drove to his own block, and left the bike. Adrenaline zapped at his heart, like a frog's tongue at a fly. Bounding up the stairs, he flung his door wide, walked from room to room.

Margy wasn't home. A peach, half eaten, rotted on the music stand. The bed was an explosion, pillows flung and sheets erupted in waves, sprawled on the floor. He put his nose down to the sheets, saw faint brown stains. His heart began to thunder in his ears.

He found her calendar, nothing on it for today. Underneath it, casually flipped back, the rehearsal schedule for Ravinia. Today there was no rehearsal, no program. But three nights ago, they'd played Tchaikovsky and Rachmaninoff, with a piano soloist. Michael Sein, it said. Michael Sein, the Bagworm, who had done things to her Webster would not think about. He would not. She hadn't even mentioned that the Bagworm was in town.

His mind shut to a pinhead, thoughtless as a creature with no brain. On instinct, cerebellum, his hand found the phone, punched Calvin's number. Calvin had probably gone out with his gay friends, none of whom conformed to anything Webster thought he knew about gay men. They wore jeans and flannel shirts, trooped around like lumberjacks, maybe talked a little too much on the phone. Two of them were portly guys about

fifty who drove a big-wheel pickup, had brown teeth and cau-
liflower ears, looked prepared to lynch the only gay man ever
seen in Lubbock, Texas. But they'd been lovers thirty years.
Once when Webster went downstairs to look for Margy, a
young man he'd never seen before came to Calvin's door. Tall
and dark, broad-shouldered in a black T-shirt and jeans, he
looked more or less like Webster, who also happened to have
on a black T-shirt and jeans. The young man's glance swept
down his shoulders, belly, crotch, then back up to his eyes,
ending in a soul-divining gaze.

"Margy," Webster managed to say. The young man stepped
aside.

"Too bad," he murmured as Webster passed.

～

Calvin wasn't home. His machine picked up, gave a serious
greeting about the Men's Emergency Health Network, which
he had organized since half his friends had lately come down
with strange cancers, or stomach parasites that usually affected only sheep. The greeting was long, detailed, gave as-
signments to the volunteers, and Webster did not listen to the
end. Clearly, Calvin was no help. Hanging up, he removed all
signs that he had been home and vanished down the stairs.

Rolling the bike a few blocks off, he hid it under a tarp. It was an August afternoon, the sky shellacked, the sort of day when old people expired on sidewalks, trying to reach shade, and teenaged fathers shook their infant sons to death. Across the street from their building, in a finger of the park, drug dealers loitered by the public phones. A game of vicious basketball surged back and forth across the courts, one team all black, the other white. Webster found a spot under a tree, where he could guard his back and watch his front door without being seen.

He didn't have to wait long. Margy's car flashed up the block. Driving fast, impatiently, the way she always did, she accelerated till the last second and slammed on the brakes. The only open spot along the block was by the hydrant, and she whipped into it, shrugged out of the car as if it were a negligee she let drop to the floor. Her hair was like a mustard field in bloom, her round breasts bounced as she clicked up the sidewalk in high heels. Her black skirt barely reached her thighs, blue circles underneath her eyes. Were those fingerprints all over her? Clacking to their building, she swung her hips, loose-boned, as if she didn't care who knew.

Ten minutes later she was back, with the slouchy shoulder bag she used to carry concert clothes, though she wasn't going to a concert now. She must have needed clean underwear, more birth control. Tossing it into the car, she drove quickly away.

Webster had to sprint, but he stayed half a block behind her yellow car, trotting in place when she stopped at a light. His eyes had recently gone bad, using computers in the lab. In the average wolf pack now, he would be left behind to starve. But he was lucky, since she stayed on crowded streets, not turning out to Lake Shore Drive, and he could keep up well enough to watch her twirl her hair around one finger, chew her nails, beat time to the radio on her car door. Parking at a drugstore, she came out with a plastic bag, then made complicated turns through residential streets, slowed to a creep.

Finally she left the car, a half block from the park, not far from their own place. It was a nice block, flowers in the yards, elegant old brownstones blasted clean, with potted plants that trailed from balconies. From behind a large oak tree, he watched her use a key on the front door of one and disappear inside it with the plastic bag.

Streaming with sweat, he leaned his wet face on the tree's rough bark. For a long time he managed not to think. He checked the bark for ants. There should be ants here, but there weren't, just as spiders didn't blow in the windows of his apartment house. He could just leave Chicago. He didn't even have to tell her where he went. Oh, God, what was in that plastic bag? Condoms, sponges, foam. How long had she been doing this? It was the basic rule of field-sighting. For every one you saw, there were a hundred you did not.

Knees stiff from standing, he walked up and down the block, not caring who saw him. Peering through the window of the brownstone foyer, he tried to read the mailbox names but couldn't see in the dim light. Inside, a door closed.

"Careful," said a voice that might be Margy's.

Lurching to a run, he loped the half block to the park, willing himself to keep going. Did he really want to know? But his feet would not go on. He had to look.

The front door of the brownstone opened slowly, and the two of them came out. The man was tall and dark, and draped around her shoulders, Margy's bright hair massed against his black T-shirt. One of her arms clung tightly around him, hand no doubt in the back pocket of his jeans. They drifted toward the stairs, slow as in a dream. Oh, it was a cozy scene, cozy. Did he kiss her like he meant it? Fuck her, of course she meant. Fuck her, with sincerity.

She bent down, took hold of the man's knee, lifted his foot, set it on the stair below. She picked up the other leg, braced herself against the rail. The guy lost interest in the operation. His eyes wandered, found Webster's down the block, and fastened onto them. Webster took a step back toward the trees. Where had he seen that look? On a man with wider shoulders, cheeks more full? Now he looked gaunt and pale. Ill. But still it was a soul-divining gaze.

~

Nothing looked the same. The whole street rearranged itself. Webster rushed toward them.

"Margy, my God."

"You never listen to me," she said mildly, reintroducing him to Todd. Todd lifted a stiff finger, waggled it at him, scolding. One side of his face looked slightly bent. He couldn't seem to talk. Margy's small arms held him, and her face looked soft.

"Todd was a wee bit forgetful about how to walk after his meningitis. But now look at him. He's a champ."

Webster walked around the park with them. No drug dealers appeared. Old women in babushkas nattered together on benches, in Polish, Serb, or Croat. A young woman walked a Great Dane bigger than a calf. Light seemed to pour from Margy's hair. Margy, his wife! Not lost! A man who looked Armenian, in a brown suit, walked toward them carrying a baby in a party dress. All these people seemed to know the secret of happiness.

Margy touched his arm. "You're shivering. You're soaking wet. Did you run in these clothes?"

He shrugged. He wasn't cold. But he let her send him home. The apartment seemed to glow, while he showered, put away her shoes. Making the bed, he bent to smooth the sheet and saw her chart, tucked under the mattress. Unfolding it, he checked. Her temperature had spiked the day before, right on schedule, day fourteen. It meant a live egg was at large, packed with fifty billion years of evolution, Margy's music talent, green eyes, frothy hair. Prickling swept Webster's back, as if a bed of nails had been applied to it, briefly. The timing didn't mean a thing, of course. It was only a coincidence. He made the bed.

He heard her coming up the stairs, rattling a grocery sack. She dropped her keys, sang bits of opera. Her voice was low and smoky, but trained from years of music school, so she could hit the right notes, hold up both ends of an intricate Mozart duet.

"*Là ci darem la mano. Vorrei e non vorrei . . .*"

Her heels kept time, click, click, *sprezzatura* on the hardwood floor, up the hall toward him.

He stood in the middle of the living room, too agitated to sit down. When she saw him, she stopped and tipped her head.

"What's the matter, sweetie? Your hair's standing on end." Shifting the groceries to one arm, she reached up, tried to smooth it down.

He took the sack from her and set it on the floor. He put his arms around her, pressed his nose into her hair.

"Sweetheart. Would one child satisfy you?" He felt himself quiver, from somewhere in his abdomen.

She laughed. "Is that a theoretical question?"

He watched this scene from eight or nine feet in the air, the guy down on the floor some other man.

"It's an offer, I think."

She pulled her head back, frowned. "How long have you been thinking about this?"

"About five seconds. If I thought about it longer, I'd be too afraid."

She gave him a flashing grin. "I don't suppose you've seen my chart."

"I have, actually."

"Better watch what you offer."

"I know exactly what I'm offering."

Laughing, tipping back her head, she lifted his hand and looked at it. Casually, as if she wasn't doing anything, she started strolling up the hall. His breath rasped in his ears. He couldn't hear. The walk was too short. By the bed, he paused.

"I'm not sure I recall the procedure here."

She took his T-shirt off, his jeans. He could remember everything he'd ever read by Kierkegaard, Camus. Someday this kid would ask why it was born. Why was it here? What was the purpose of its birth? It would grow old, lose what it loved, feel pain, and die. Webster wilted, not yet inside.

"Stage fright," he said, grimacing.

She chuckled. "Look at it this way. It's not your body on the line. It isn't you who's never going to be the same. You could do this ten times a day across the countryside, and not be changed."

Possibly not ten. But that was all he needed now. Resuming, he waited for the tornado that usually arrived to whirl away the feel of their bodies. But this time a big light in his brain switched on. He knew exactly where her skin met his, thighs around his hips, tissues parted slippery. He could calibrate each upward ratchet of his heart, hydraulic rushings through small tubes, valves that opened or did not, just like a motorcycle speeding toward a cliff, wind in their faces, lots of

time to swerve aside, they couldn't fly, the cliff too high, the
air too thin, how could they fling themselves out into it? Then
they were in the air, her head thrown back, his face pressed to
her neck, his body pinned on top of hers, both of them crying
out, about to plummet to the ground.

～

They did not make love again for weeks.

Diarrhea, Webster thought as he opened his eyes. The only
time he had ever taken care of a baby, it was a huge boy with
the runs, and it kept wobbling to its feet, giving him a tooth-
less grin while huge dollops of yellow shit dropped to the
floor from its exhausted diapers. He tried to change them, but
it got up and careened around the room, emitting happy
shrieks, tipped over chairs and lamps. He looked around their
small apartment now. Where should he begin? Buy rubber
sheets? Bolt down the furniture?

Margy seemed to shine, with a moist radiance, like a
lightning bug. Humming, she stopped by his chair to kiss his
head. One afternoon, when he came home from the lab, a T-
shirt and jeans lay on the bed, no bigger than his hands. They
appeared to be a person's clothes. A person with arms and
legs, another person in their home. A fat kid with small eyes,

riding in the back seat of the car, disapproving of their every move.

"Jesus, Dad, you call that a *haircut?*"

"Yeah, my dad's a scientist, *sort of.*"

Two excruciating weeks oozed by, one millisecond at a time. Margy had a textbook cycle, always the same. Furtively he checked her chart. It was day fifteen, then sixteen, twenty-one. Twenty-five, when would it end? Twenty-seven, twenty-eight at last. Then twenty-nine. Thirty, thirty-one, dread cresting up like nausea. In the bathroom cabinet, the tampons disappeared, replaced by a new box, lurid pink. Seven days after missed period, ten drops of urine in the tube, stir with the stick.

In the mirror she admired her breasts, already bigger, sore. On their way to huge. She laughed, holding them.

"The Irish are very fertile. My mom got pregnant four times in three years. She could conceive from a sultry look. Of course, she lost the other three. She couldn't stay pregnant, till me." Margy looked more sober, as if starting to brood.

On the morning of day thirty-two, she kissed his back as he got out of bed, put her arms around him from behind.

"Don't ever let me throw you away," she said.

Webster was arrested in the middle of a yawn. Was it up to him? Was she thinking of it?

"Okay," he said, and waited till she let him go before he stood up, pulled on jeans, loaded his pack. He was especially busy now, collating data from his trip, plus giving extra hours to the frogs. The university was all the way across the city, on the Southside, and he had to leave early to beat the traffic, stay down till late at night, stare at a computer screen until he couldn't see across the room. Sometimes he didn't make it home till Margy was asleep.

Day thirty-three, after almost three sexless weeks, he stayed in the lab long after everyone was gone, and masturbated quietly on his lab stool. Margy was too close to think of, and mixed up now with yellow babyshit. Instead he saw his first girlfriend, whose father had spotted a footprint on the chimney, planted there one muddy night as Webster shoved his way into her room. Then the new student in his lab, who must be all of twenty-two, some awful name like Tiffany. She watched him with sad eyes, brought over slides and asked, could he help her? Silky hair slid past her neck, and earrings tinkled, blouse gapped at her breasts as she bent down to watch what he was showing her.

He caught some on a slide, used the big lab microscope. Thrashing was all he saw at first, lots of mobility. No hope of failure there. He focused in on one of them, nothing but a tail and a wish. Was he supposed to live its life? The rest of him just legs and feet to carry it around, get it properly injected, build a nest?

"Salmon, squid, all that stuff spawns and dies," he told the creatures on the slide. He washed them off.

～

Lights burned in the living room when he got home, violin case in the corner by the couch. But she was not in any room. Checking the kitchen counters for a note, he picked up the phone and started to punch Calvin's number when he heard a small sound like a gasp. Following it up the hall, he tried the bedroom, then the bath.

She was in the empty tub, clothes on. His eyes adjusted to the dark. He saw a small box, not the new one but the old kind, blessed blue, tampons. Wings unfurled in his chest. Flinging aside the shower curtain, he put his arms around her in the cold tub, picked her up.

"Sweetheart," he said. "Sweetheart."

Carrying her to the bed, he folded around her. She felt so good! He pressed in close and put his nose against her head. She smelled warm, a little acrid, sweet.

"You bastard," she said.

He was just hauling in a breath, and he went ahead and finished it. Okay. Okay, sure. He could feel it now, her skin clenched like starfish armor, *Echinodermata*, spiny to the touch. He pulled back to look at her.

"Why, exactly?"

Even in the dark, her eyes were fierce.

"Oh, come on. One grand gesture, as if that means anything. And then you were so cold to me. What would have happened in another month? You would have *slept* at the lab by then."

His head hurt suddenly. He rubbed his forehead, but it didn't help.

"I tried to give you what you wanted."

That wasn't the whole story, but it was part of it. How could he explain? It was as if he had been tricked, or tricked himself, and then the trick had stopped.

She searched his face. "I didn't want to do it by myself. I thought if I just waited a few years . . . Men want children too, don't they, when they grow up?"

Name two, he might have said. But he could name them himself. Whole cultures of them, chanting on the evening news, demanding six sword-waving sons. Muslims, Hindus, Baptists, Mormons, Catholics, all responding to some urge he didn't feel, to swim upstream, be fruitful, multiply, make four where there were two, then six or eight or twelve, a baseball team of one man's progeny. The pope traveled the world, saying a special mass for women who had borne fifteen, answering the call of God. Which God exactly, though? The one that made the manatee, the snow leopard, the dodo bird?

He felt staked to the bed. "We can do it, if you want. But I can't make myself want to. It doesn't work like that."

She lay crumpled next to him. An hour seemed to pass. Then her body settled, like a door clicked closed. She looked calm, relaxed. Reaching out one hand, she gave his chest a pat, once, twice, with finality.

It was a tiny gesture, but something lifted off in him. He was not such a bad guy! He was a friend to jellyfish, freshwater shrimp, and frogs. He'd given life a chance. Life had its own reasons, and he would keep an eye on them. Raising his arm, the way he always did, he made room for her against his chest and waited for her to roll toward him.

Last of the Genuine Castrati

~~~~~~~~

Down the hill, the city of Dante and Michelangelo wavered in the heat, red tile, and ocher clay, Duomo rising like a mushroom cloud of stone. Margy picked up the hotel phone, tapped in her former number in Chicago. Waiting, she could see a gray hair, curled into a question mark beside her face. Carefully, she yanked it out. The phone began to ring a quarter of the way around the globe. As a child, she had thought the sound you heard was the real ring of a phone in someone's home. Now she knew that it was just a buzzing on the line and would sound the same after the house burned down.

"Hello," Webster said evenly.

She felt a rush of affection that almost strangled her. They had been married for six years, and she had left him a month ago. "Oh, hi, sweetie. What are you doing?"

It was early morning in Chicago, and he'd be rushing to the lab. He might be naked, fresh out of the shower, body lean and graceful as an arrow shot from a bow. He had skin like silk above the nipples on his chest.

"I can't talk right now," he said mournfully.

"I'm sorry. It's seven there, right? Thought I might catch you before you left."

He grunted. His voice had a desperate quality. "I haven't left. But I can't talk."

"Why? What's happening?"

She tried to keep her voice even and calm. When he was crying, desperate, it seemed to help. Sometimes he called her in the middle of the night to say he'd die if she did not come back to him. One time he said he was kneeling in the bathtub, holding a knife. She talked him into dropping it and calling friends.

Now he sounded desperate in a different way.

"Good-bye," he whispered, and she heard the creak of a door opening in his apartment, the sound of footsteps on the hardwood floor, light and quick, like a young girl in summer flats.

"Is there someone in the apartment?" Margy gasped.

Webster whispered woefully, "Yes."

"Who is it?"

"Tiffany."

Margy hung up. She picked up the receiver, slammed it down again. Some kind of poison poured through all her veins and arteries. He sounded fine, he sounded almost . . . happy.

"Don't worry, someday someone else will love you," she'd said a month ago, as she stood in the doorway with her suitcase and her violin. She had even patted his arm. She was so sure she was going off with James, who was English and the violist in a quartet she'd lately joined. The quartet would play its European tour, and then she'd live with James and have six kids. She worried about Webster, kindly, as a friend. She felt relieved on the long flight to London and for at least five cities on the tour. She slept with James, and talked to Webster several times a day. It was only the adjustment, she thought. They were going to be fine.

The arched stone window let in whiffs of jasmine and chlorine and horse dung. In the drive below, a Florentine policeman loitered, dressed in gleaming white on a black horse. The hotel had been a convent in the fifteenth century, made of stone. Other women used to stand here in this window, looking out. Did anything feel simpler to them? One morning in the kitchen, Webster had bent to kiss her, and she realized she couldn't see him anymore. She saw his face the way she did her own, with recognition, only not from the outside, the way it felt when she looked in a mirror. Did that have to mean she was connected to him, underneath, forever and ever, world without end?

The policeman shifted and gazed up at her. The saddle creaked. He looked bored, looked away.

~~

She couldn't take a tranquilizer now. The quartet had a concert in four hours, and she had to be able to pick up the bow. They played recent compositions and baroque, Beethoven and plane crashes for strings, with titles like "Scarecrow Eats His Liver in the Morning," a lot of Philip Glass. The other three were probably asleep, or meditating, trying to stay calm.

Not that anyone was going to come to hear them play. It turned out they were scheduled at the same time as a musical sensation sweeping Italy. Emilio Gentille had a high soprano range, so sweet and true that he was rumored not to be a modern countertenor, merely trained, but rather the old-fashioned kind, vocal cords undamaged by testosterone. He was said to sing like a cathedral choirboy, with the power of a grown man's lungs, pure as temple bells in Himalayan air. That night he planned to do the rarest Buxtehude cantatas, and Florence churned with fans, frantic for seats. Paparazzi milled alertly outside all the best hotels, while police stood guard and vans pulled up with wreaths of lilies and gardenias big enough to drape a horse.

Margy put on her bathing suit and shorts and running shoes. Since leaving Webster, she had felt a need to leap tall buildings at a single bound. Her blood seemed turned into adrenaline. She didn't sleep. She worked out all the time.

Dashing out the back of the hotel, she ran across a terrace by the pool, where three paparazzi sat with cameras, smoking. Glancing up, they looked away. Another American violinist, so what.

At the bottom of the garden, old rock steps sank toward Florence, through olive groves and crackling grass and foxtails. Wisteria held up stone walls, leaves dull with dust and wilted in the blazing sun. She ran down to the city's edge and up again, down, up, Sisyphean, till sweat leaked stinging into her eyes.

"Do re me fa sol la ti do," she sang under her breath. She was calm. Her husband was not fucking anyone.

"This little piggy had roast beef. This little piggy had none."

Zing, a horsefly bit her shoulder. Throwing off her shorts, she dove into the pool, swam furiously back and forth.

～

Back in her room, chlorine and sweat mixed in a sticky layer on her skin. The message light flashed on the phone. Webster had a lot of nerve if he thought she wanted to hear from him! She dialed the message line.

"Emergency meeting, bridal suite," it said.

Deflated, she sank into a chair. In every city they had played, James had booked himself into the bridal suite under fake names. He was trying to hide from his ex-wife, who was Sicilian and determined, he felt sure, to put a dagger in his heart. In Milan, he registered as Signor and Signora Verdi, and in Venice as the newlywed Puccinis. In Verona, warily, he changed the theme, to Mr. and Mrs. Greenleaf Whittier. His ex-wife lived in Florence, and he tried to convince the rest of them to drop it from the tour. When he couldn't, he barricaded himself in the bridal suite, where he was Thomas Love Peacock and bride, and had not left once since they arrived.

She did not call him back. She had something to say to Webster first. Tapping the number in Chicago, she waited. The machine did not pick up. Webster must have turned it off, but she knew it would switch on at the sixteenth ring. Waiting patiently, she heard the clicks and whirrs. There was a new greeting. His taped voice sounded cheerful—in fact, exuberant.

"Hi, this is Web. Isn't this a great day? One of the best! Please, please leave me a message, okay?"

Web? No one had ever called him that. He was too dignified, and he almost never sounded this excited about anything. Something was very wrong.

She punched in the code for remote retrieval of the messages. *Beep, beep, whir, click,* said the machine. The tape rewound with ratlike squeaks.

"Hi, babe," said a young woman's voice. "It's Tiff. Just got your message, and I want to say, you make me so happy. It was, like, *totally* worth it to wait for you, and I can hardly wait till you get over here. We'll get in bed and stay in there for days. We won't go out at all. We'll just peek in the fridge for nibbles and get back in bed. We'll be wiped out together all the time. Won't it be ecstasy? Love ya." *Beep beep beep.*

Margy threw the phone onto the bed. Her wrists were strapped in carpal-tunnel splints, and she was not supposed to pound on anything. She smashed it with a pillow, *whump whump whump.*

Collapsing next to it, she sobbed. She was not in love with Webster! She had left him. She had to be in love with James—that was decided, finished with. Of course Webster was moving on. He'd found another woman, a girl really, one of the students in his lab. So what? So he had Tiffany, and she had James.

She sobbed so hard her abdomen went into spasm, jerking her upright. It was like a giant hiccup, or a sit-up, ten, twelve, twenty times. At first it felt good, like dancing, or some strange aerobic exercise. Then it began to hurt. But it would not stop. She was a cog inside a clock, a piece by Philip Glass, two hundred forty repetitions of the same arpeggio.

"Oh, oh," she said and jerked upright. "Oh, oh."

~

She washed her face and smoothed her hair. Calmly, she walked down to the bridal suite. She did a knock James would recognize, in six-eight time.

"Signor Peacock?"

He didn't answer, but it only meant he didn't want to let his voice be heard. She tried the door, and it swung open to a large and sunny room, brilliant green and yellow floor of serpentine limestone. Under arched windows stood the monstrous bed, white ruffles flounced with eyelet and ribbon rosettes.

James lay in the middle of it with a lit Gauloise. He was big and fair and rosy, with small black moles like brushstrokes underneath his eyes that made him look somewhat depraved ("kissed by a fairy," he liked to say). His Oxford shirt was un-buttoned, and she could see the thick scar that circled his chest, from having half a lung removed. He was only thirty-six, but padded like an older man, and he smoked Gauloises, or Players, or Pall Malls, and drank chilled gin with rumors of vermouth. His idea of a green vegetable was avocado stuffed with crab and mayonnaise, two bottles of champagne. As he sat up, ice cubes tinkled in his glass.

"Shut that door at once," he said in his precise accent, giving every syllable its due.

Rising quickly, belly bowed out, nimble for a man his size, he tiptoed fast across the floor and flipped both locks on the door. Sweat ran to his hair ends and hung quivering like dew on leaves, milky with alcohol.

"She's here," he murmured sotto voce. "She called the hotel, talked to Dmitri. And what did he say? He *told* her I was here!"

Dmitri was their famous name, the reason people came to hear them play. In the early days of the quartet, James had offended him by watching Margy when they played, though she was only second violin. She gave James's big, broad back a pat. His shirt felt wet. She lifted off her hand.

"Well, your photograph was on the poster. Possibly that was a clue."

"Possibly," he said and smiled, looked strangely satisfied. He sat down on the bed.

"But, listen, you don't know Cia. She makes Lucretia Borgia look like the Queen Mother. Have I told you how she flung a girl downstairs because I talked to her? Have I mentioned how she slashed my bow hand with a tomato knife?"

He held the hand up and cradled it. It was his favorite myth, how Cia had been wildly jealous, listened to his phone calls, followed him when he went out. But then, he had a lot of myths. He liked to say that London Records had asked him to record Schnittke's viola concerto, though there was no recording date, and he never practiced it. Philip Glass had come to their New York debut and talked to James maybe a minute in the hall. Since then James sometimes hinted that Glass was writing a piece for him. Not the quartet, just him. He held his right hand out. There did seem to be a thin white line across the back.

"Look here and weep. She'd seen me talking to a woman in the street. It was nothing, just a moment's conversation. Do you realize what she'll do if she casts an eye on you? Don't smile! You could be dead!"

Margy sat down on the bed. "She's probably just going to hear Gentille anyway. At least she doesn't call you in the middle of the night."

Actually, Webster hadn't called for several nights. It only felt like it. She went on with energy.

"And now that fucking little girl is there with him. That little girl that he's fucking."

James smoothed wet hair out of his eyes.

"Oh, well, and why should you notice? Be happy he has a girl. Stops him coming after you with a tomato knife."

Suddenly he wrapped around her, large and damp. He pinned her on the bed.

"I'm a foxtail," he said in a fake Texas drawl, made ridiculous by his clipped English consonants. "Ah'm a foxtail, tryin' to impregnate y'all."

Panic prickled over Margy—who the hell did he sound exactly like? Someone she did not want to recall. Looking roguish, he began to flex his fingers like a cat in ecstasy. He kneaded her arm, pretending to purr. With exaggerated cat-like moves, he prowled on top of her, staring with small blue eyes.

"Some pussycats are spending too much time *yowling* and not enough time as they should. Murrrr-oww."

She made herself hold still and put her lips on his. His mouth was cold and wet. She felt a surge of anger, not desire. Gasping for air, she rose and moved away.

"Oh, God, sorry. Aren't you dying of the heat? I was just in the pool, and now I'm hot again. Let's have a swim instead. Believe me, everything is going to look better when we're cool."

〜

"James was my purple passion," Cia said, pronouncing it *poorple*, full lips pursed.

The night was clear and black with huge bright stars, and they stood on a marble terrace outside the hot room where the quartet had played. Margy gulped wine in her hot concert clothes, a miniature tuxedo made to match the rest of the quartet, black wool with pintucked shirt and studs, her hair pinned up. It had been a cute idea in January in New York, but August in Italy made them all sweat on their expensive instruments. Dmitri could be heard upstairs, raving to the impresario about the air conditioning, half in Russian, half in French. The impresario raved back in Italian.

The concert had gone fine, with almost no one there to hear, and the audience had now adjourned, to rush over the Ponte Vecchio and join the crowd around the opera house. Cia herself seemed ready to desert, but she'd politely stayed to hold one of the hundred wine glasses, pretend to nibble one of several hundred *crostini* going to waste. She was even shorter than

Margy, and plump, with creamy olive skin and lustrous black hair, big breasts almost bare inside the plunging neckline of a green silk dress. Arranging bracelets on her arms, she fixed Margy with an easy smile. She had lived with James in London and New York, and her English had a soft, round sound.

"I was lucky, I got to marry with him. Most people do not marry with their purple passion. And what about you? Who is yours? I can see you have still on your wedding ring."

Cia saluted her with her wine glass, a gesture that seemed mocking and admiring both at once. Margy slipped her other hand over the thin gold band.

"Oh, this? It's just that I'm so used to it. It feels like part of my hand. I don't wear much jewelry." She glanced at Cia's bracelets, which were gold and set with colored stones. "But those are nice. Are they from Venice?"

James stepped through the doors, talking to an older man who looked English. They both carried glasses of a clear and heavy liquid that swirled slowly as they walked. Gin fumes braced the air around them like an electronic fence.

"So you'll record it soon?" the gray-haired man said. James tucked his chin, as if trying not to brag.

"Well, not just yet. There's one or two small things that have to be—" His chin went farther down into his neck. "There's this other chap, you see. Perhaps I didn't mention it. Trying to insin-uate himself. Certain maneuverings behind the scene. Though he's not exactly—did I tell you? I saw him in London, and you see—you see, he told me London Records had asked him. And I said—I said to him—" His eyes went impish, lips pushed out as if stiff with bottled laughter. "I said—Barry?"

They walked out of range, and Cia did not turn. She smiled at Margy, dropped her voice.

"You don't have to worry about your old husband, you know. His mistress will take of him. He's fine. Don't ring his telephone if you don't want to know. James didn't even wait so long."

Margy drew herself up. She wasn't used to being taller than anyone, and it felt good. "James says he didn't sleep with other women when he was with you."

Cia tipped her head back, grinned. "And you believed him? Baa baa, little sheep, have you many wools!"

Trying to tamp down her grin, she touched Margy's wrist.

"I'm sorry, but I know my chicken. He gave me horrible dis-eases. He's going to give them to you. That's what means hus-band, you know? It means he sleeps with other women too."

She looked pleased and satisfied, standing square on high-heeled sandals, round feet bulging to the sides. Margy opened her mouth to say something, and closed it. That was exactly what meant husband now. At the same moment, she realized she didn't give a damn if James had been unfaithful to Cia and lied to her. She didn't even care if he slept with other women now. She only cared that Webster could be, right that minute, making love to Tiffany. She was breathless with jealousy. She smelled her concert sweat, pungent as cat pee. She took a gulp of wine.

"How long were you and James married? Was it hard to get divorced? He hasn't told me much."

Cia smiled and waved one hand. "Oh, we're still married now, of course. You didn't know? Yes, yes, we married here, in Sant' Ambrogio. You've seen it, with the little frescoes? Very nice. So you see, is no divorce for James. English divorce, ha!"

Flinging up the fingers of one hand, as if tossing rice, she laughed a lovely, pealing laugh.

"That's why Italian men are crazy for me now, with the English husband behind the coortain."

Preening, she glanced around. And it was true, nearby a young man with long hair sat smoking, watching Cia's every move. He looked through Margy's thin blond frame as if she were a palm frond in the way. Cia leaned toward her, murmuring. She smelled like strawberries and wine.

"Of course you believe him now. But, you see, he lies. Poor man, he doesn't like the truth. Has he told you yet about Philip Glass?"

Margy felt her cheeks go hot, and Cia laughed her pretty laugh again.

Abruptly James arrived and towered over them.

"We are leaving," he said, looking only at Margy. "This precise instant. We will walk toward the car."

Cia seemed to grow taller. Suddenly charged with energy, she dove for the platter of *crostini* on the table next to them.

"Here, I'll get for you," she said and minced her hips to one side as she held two out to them. "Have a nice sandwich. I'm sorry we don't have hot dogs."

James did not glance her way. He raised blond brows at Margy. His eyes bored into her.

Springing on tiptoe, Cia lifted the *crostini* to his mouth. He jerked his head away. With a lunge, she mashed it to his lips. Eyes bulging, he flashed a clean white handkerchief out of his pocket, wiped his face.

He said something in Italian, too quick for Margy's ears. Surely not that vile Italian curse about a certain type of sexual intercourse? Cia snapped back, light in her black eyes.

"*Questa*," she said and gestured with her whole arm at Margy. "*Questa, questa*" something. Could it be *farfalla?* James's voice rolled lyrically, not English in the least. He seemed to call Cia a bird of prey.

"*E tu, uccello sanguinario!* What a beautiful disguise!"

Cia tossed her hair back, spoke quite clearly.

"The angels go naked," she said and fired off something much too quick. Margy stood beside them, felt a spray of spit. Neither of them seemed to notice when she walked away.

~~

"Oh, Christ, there she is again!" His voice shot up. "Quick, over there!"

Margy looked, but saw only the front of the hotel, where men with cameras surged back and forth like soccer fans, trampling the jasmine and azaleas. A searchlight zigzagged, dazzling, on the stone walls. James perched on the limo seat, tense as a string about to snap.

"Driver! *Ragazzo, prego!* We can't stay here tonight!"

Margy cut in, firm. "You must be hallucinating. Do you realize you see her everywhere? Isn't that the definition of obsession?"

"Oh, I see, it's I who am obsessed. By all means, stay here
if you like, and call up Webster all night long. See if anyone
believes you're not obsessed!"

"Me! That's ridiculous!"

James laughed. "Don't mind me. Of course I've never understood what you could possibly have seen in him. Cretin
that he is . . ."

"Cia *waddles* when she walks," she hissed.

Three men with klieg lights rushed the car. In a moment,
the whole crowd surrounded them. James moved, calm and
stately, to a dark corner up by the driver's seat. Bowing, he
swept one hand to point her toward the door.

"Fine," said Margy. "Go ahead and run from your chimera.
Have a nice evening."

Clutching her violin, she stepped out into exploding
lights. The paparazzi all looked devastated and confused.

"Ah, *signora, signora*," one moaned and shook his head as if
she had betrayed some code of decency. Haggard, with a
skinny neck, he trembled violently.

~~

Every composer had a tune he couldn't shake. Beethoven's
"Ode to Joy" broke out in other choruses, Vivaldi's "Four Sea-

sons" leaked into his cello concerto. Gershwin never quite got free of "Summertime." Margy went up to her room, took off her wedding ring. Obsessed? Obsessed with Webster? Worms on the ocean bottom learned to eat bacteria, Webster himself had told her that. Antarctic lichen learned to grow inside rocks. Other people got divorced, and so could she.

It would be afternoon in Chicago, Webster at the lab. She dialed his number anyway, to leave a message on the machine. She'd tell him she was through with him for good. He picked it up.

"I can't talk now," he said.

Flaming plutonium shot through her bones. "What are you doing, fucking in the afternoon?"

"Never mind." He hung up.

Minutes later, her phone rang.

"Margy," he said mournfully. It had a different sound, as if he'd rushed out to a pay phone on the street.

"Webster. Where'd you leave the little girl? Did you tell her you were going out to walk the dog?"

"Ice cream," he said in a tone of woe.

"I bet she's dumb enough to believe that—"

"You keep your mouth off her! That girl loves me, unlike you. You, who—"

"Oh, and you're so pure. Why did you sneak out to call me? Is that what you're really like? I suppose I didn't know what you were doing all along. I have news for you. I'm not the other woman. I'm your wife."

"The hell you are. You never were, not for a day. You lied to me, right from the start. You lie and lie—"

"*I* lie? How long have you had a taste for teenagers? That's what you want—" They were both screaming now.

"Oh yes, look who you picked. English scum—"

"A baby bimbo—"

"Moral maggot—"

"She's no threat to your—"

"You slut—"

"You adolescent—"

She had no idea she could hit a note like that. She sounded like a pipe organ, and so did he. It was a duet for screams, obscene as what you heard of the insane. They subsided, breathing hard. Nobody hung up.

Expensive moments passed.

"Where are you?" she said quietly. "On the corner by the ice cream store?"

He sighed. "Just down the block, on Clark. I can see our building, sort of. It's blurred."

"Why don't you go to the eye doctor? Don't you want to see?" She felt a rush of tenderness. "You should take better care of yourself."

"I've decided that a little blur improves the look of things."

"The Impressionists were all myopic. It expressed their inner being. Maybe yours too."

"Maybe. I've been plenty myopic." His voice tightened, slid up several tones. "So, were they all cuckolds? Did Madame Monet let her bloomers down for everyone?"

Slam, went a door in Margy's chest. "Where did you leave the bimbo, anyway? In bed, keeping your spot warm?"

"Don't call her that, all right? Don't call her anything—"

"You think you can just call me up, and then go back home to your little—"

"I said shut up about her!"

"Inflatable doll—"

"She's a saint beside—"

"With her soap-opera name—"

"Your gigolo—"

"Shut up! Shut up! Am I supposed to kill myself, or what?"

~~

She went down to the bridal suite. It wasn't locked, and James was gone. The bridal suite gave her the creeps, but she borrowed a bottle of his gin and took it back up to her room, poured it in a bathroom glass. She washed a tranquilizer down with the first glass, and poured another one.

Sweet smells of sage came lilting in her windows on the downhill side, and she sat in front of them, while the lights of Florence glowed like candle flames, unwavering in the warm air. Of course James was right. She was mixed up with Webster in some way she didn't understand. She seemed to love him, actually, and now she had arranged to hand him over to someone else. Way to go, Margy. He'd probably get married, even have a kid. He certainly would not come back to her. What was she going to do? She wasn't sure. She drank more gin.

Pushing a window open wide, she wound up her right arm and pitched the wedding ring out as far as it would go. It seemed the healthy thing to do. That was it, the end.

She took a sleeping pill and felt a rosy moist sensation, like the inside of a tiger's mouth. It seemed to be a sort of happiness. She wrote herself a note, in French, the only language she could recall. *Il faut être toujours ivre. Toujours dancent au bout de précipice.* She did some leaps she'd learned in elementary school ballet. The floor seemed portable, flew up to meet her cheek.

She dreamed she was back home in Chicago, carrying a suitcase. She had been to Europe, not with James but with Michael Sein. He followed her inside and watched her take a shower, sitting on the toilet seat, shower curtain clear as glass. The door opened, and Webster walked in.

"Look who's here!" she cried and leaped out of the shower, trying to smooth over the awkwardness of the situation. She opened her suitcase, and a wolf came out. It was only a small wolf, but it ate Webster, and her mother and father. Chunks of flesh lay across the hardwood floor in pools of blood.

"Unnhhhhh! Unnhhhhh!"

She tried to scream, but couldn't move her tongue.

~~

The pain in her wrists woke her. The splints were off, her hands bent hard, like a coma patient's in the fetal position. She couldn't seem to move. Her head felt big as the Duomo and just as hollow, echoing. Lifting it an inch, she crawled into the marble bathroom, retched into the marble toilet, cheek resting against the seat.

It seemed to take an hour to get into shorts, T-shirt. Shoes she couldn't manage, and she crept barefoot down the cold stone stairs. The hotel felt enclosed in sleep, dust motes float-ing in the early light.

Outside, the sun already blazed, the sky a vicious blue, horseflies circling the pool. Stomach lurching, she made her way around the back, into the garden underneath her win-dow, where she knelt to comb her fingers slowly through the dirt in beds of jasmine and azaleas, around a fountain, under cypress trees. Ornamental hedges scratched her arms. She did not find the ring.

A yellow bird flew past, wings with black-and-white stripes like a huge butterfly. Landing on a wall, it raised its spiky yellow crown at her, like the Statue of Liberty. Webster would have known its name, but she couldn't ask him any-more. Sitting in the dust under a cypress tree, she was too de-hydrated to cry. *Zing*, a horsefly bit her neck. She slapped it and began to bleed.

She made her way back up the slippery steps. Inside, at the second floor, she had to pass the bridal suite. Maybe she should see if James had gotten back all right. He might be passed out in the piazza, under Perseus, or on some bridge over the Arno. James was not so bad. She would just have a look at him, and see how she felt. He was not fat really, just big and flamboyant like the fifteenth-century marble heroes

lounging in fountains all over Italy. When he slept, he lay
sprawled out, pink face creased like a glove thrown down, one
big arm dangling out into the air.

She tried the knock he knew, but there was no reply.
Pressing her ear against the grainy oak, she couldn't hear a
thing. She took hold of the brass knob, gave it a turn.

Sunlight scorched the white bride's bed. At first she could
not see, the bed too bright, like a mirage. Then two figures
emerged, one large and pink, a scar around its chest, the other
short and round with bracelets on its arms. Heads near the
door, they faced each other, almost not touching, while their
hips pulsed in and out like waves, only the purple shaft of penis
in between. A rush of breath, a gentle suck and smack. They
could be starfish in a pool, or snails connected by hermaphro-
ditic arms. They could be jets in space, the bigger one maneuvering a tube to inject fuel into the smaller as they flew.

She watched them from two yards away, and they did not
glance at her, or pause. Backing out the door, she tried to ease
it closed. But it stuck on the old stone floor and squealed
across it like the little piggy that cried *wee wee wee* all the way
home.

Risk

~~~~~~~~~~

Margy and Webster needed a vacation, after the year they'd had. After the year they'd had, they couldn't afford one, but that didn't worry them. Nothing further, they decided, was going to worry them. Their apartment had been broken into twice, but they didn't look for anyone to stay in it. Payments on Margy's violin were twice their rent, but they left it inside. They packed the credit cards, turned out the lights, and didn't even bother to close the blinds.

They got onto an aging DC-10 and flew to San Francisco, where an earthquake, possibly major, was predicted to happen within five days. In those five days they slept in a room on the nineteenth floor, drank in revolving bars atop tall buildings floating on landfill, and idled in traffic on the lower decks of freeways and on bridges over the bay. In a new rental car, with no replacement insurance, they took a drive along the San Andreas Fault and parked near a fissure that had swallowed a cow in 1906. They hiked the crumbling coastal mountains, on paths made famous by the Trailside Killer, and loitered on the edge of a sandstone cliff that had once slid sixteen feet in forty-five seconds, watching seals cavort in the ocean below.

They ate sushi without inspecting it, though a man in Webster's lab was studying the worm that lives in raw fish and digs into the human stomach, from which it must be surgically removed. They drove to a deserted headlands parking lot at midnight, left their wallets in the car under a sign saying not to do that, slid down a narrow path through poison oak and rattlesnakes by moonlight to a secluded beach, and swam in the icy waters where a great white shark had eaten a swimmer in 1964. They drove to Yosemite and carried backpacks up ten thousand feet, though altitude made Webster sick, could leave him retching on the trail, unable to walk, and they timed the trip to see the full moon in eclipse, though Margy was having her period, and bears in other parks had killed menstruating women. They slept on the ground in a tent and did not hang their food in a tree. The moon rose, shimmering white, and tinted bloodstain red.

"We seem to be taking our chances here," they noticed, everywhere they went. They didn't mind, so long as they were holding hands. They had yet to pay the phone bills from their months apart, which came to several thousand dollars by themselves, plus airfare back and forth to Europe several times, therapy for both of them and Tiffany, another ten thousand that they could not account for at all. It might be years before they made it into the black.

But they were back together, and happier than they had ever been. Breaking up had cleared the air, and they could fall in love again. Nothing else was going to worry them. Was that a mossy rock on the brink of a high waterfall? A hidden beach, soon to be cut off by the advancing tide?

"Now, there's an inviting spot," they said. "Let's go over there and check that out."

And they clutched hands, and kissed each other, and looked for some new way to risk their lives.

∼

On their last day in California, having exhausted the possibilities for disaster, they called old friends who had lately moved to Berkeley. David had been Webster's friend since MIT, and until lately he and his wife had lived in Lincoln Park, close enough for Webster to stumble through the streets and throw himself tragically on their carpet. He had not seen them since getting back together with Margy. He had sent a postcard, saying they were coming west, but he'd put off calling until now.

"We've rebuilt our marriage from the ground up," he said on the phone, trying to sound relaxed. He remembered other calls he'd made to them, like the night he took a hatchet to Margy's clothes. When he had them all in pieces, the Belle France skirts, weeping and tearing silky fabric with his teeth, the winter coats, the high heels, all the miniskirts, he put his head into the oven, took it out, and called David and Isa.

"The main thing is," he told them now, "the main thing is, we're all right. I mean, we're better than all right. Things are better than they've ever been. Of course there might have been a better way to do it, something less confusing for our friends. But that was the way we did it, and therefore, in the Zen sense or something, the way it had to be done."

David and Isa sounded wary. But they agreed to meet them for a peripatetic dinner, progressing course by course through Berkeley restaurants. Margy felt a little wary too, crossing the Bay Bridge. How much did David and Isa know about the year they'd had? How much had Webster said?

He would not have told them why she left. Not the big

reason, and not the little ones, the years of all his small hysterias. Once he forbade her to go to a free car wash, because even for free it pampered the car. He refused to buy products in plastic or let Margy kill a bug. If an ant came into their apartment, Webster fed it, made a house for it, while spiders fattened overhead, sent offspring through the air on tiny filaments. Once he kept a housefly as a pet, closing it in the guest room, where it lived in safety for several weeks, since it was winter and the spiders were asleep. Flies are losing ground, he said. The human race is already redundant. Once he said he'd leave her if she got pregnant.

"Sweetheart," she said, glancing back and forth expertly from him to the road. She did most of the driving, since she was better at it, and cared more. Webster didn't care what lane they were in, or how to get where they were going. He had no sense of direction, and his eyes were bad at night, when the thickness of his new contacts warped his view of the oncoming lights. Fingers lightly but alertly on the wheel, she glanced at him. "Sweetheart, how much do David and Isa know?"

Webster was looking down, examining his tie, which Margy had bought for him. It was sage-green silk with a 1920s print, and a little on the lavish side. But when Margy had broken his heart, he'd made a remarkable discovery, that women noticed him more often when he wore a tie. All he had to do was walk down the street in one, and every young woman he passed gave him a searching look. Here was a man of substance, a tie must say to them, like the courtship displays of certain birds, who puffed up the orange air sacs in their necks, did backflips over branches, turned their feathers inside out. Here was a man who could build a fine nest. Had other men noticed that ties had that effect? He should bring it up to David if he got the chance.

"How much do they know?" he said and smoothed his tie.

"You know," she said and tried to catch his eye.

He blinked to resettle his contacts, get them into position so he could focus on her. Tonight she had her hair in springy ringlets, a way he liked. It made her look about eight, playing in a grown-up dress. She could pretend to be a full-sized human, but he knew the truth. He folded her clothes out of the dryer, tiny shirts and socks, underpants the size of his hand. Lying on her back in bed, she didn't make a bump in the comforter.

He batted some ringlets around. "I know what, Mouse?"

She ducked. "Hey." She'd spent an hour in rollers with the dryer, getting out the frizz.

"You know. About this year. I suppose they heard about my glorious behavior?"

"Oh, well."

Grimly he looked out the window. Of course he'd talked to David about what she had done. "You are the victim of a terrorist attack," David had said, and he was right. Margy believed she could have what she wanted, no matter how impossible or who got hurt, and that life was full of second chances. She arrived at airports when her plane was due to leave and ran gaily through the terminal, waving her ticket overhead. She planted peonies in October and felt betrayed when they were under snow. Her credit cards were a disaster. Living with Margy, he had gotten in the habit of forgiving her. He could get off a plane and wait for her to meet him, just an hour late. He could try to understand when she left him for another man. He could let her drive. That was the secret of marriage, he'd come to realize. You had to stop yourself from clutching the wheel when your wife turned her back to the traffic, trying to look you in the eye.

"Don't worry," he said and focused on the road ahead, hoping she would do the same. He patted her thigh. "When they see how happy we are, they'll forget the whole thing."

～

David and Isa met them at Christopher's, where they started with rock shrimp, hearts of palm, a bottle of Pinot Blanc—

though Isa, who was usually fond of wine, drank mineral water. She also wore a sari, which was odd. She'd been in the States since high school, and usually she wore loafers and pleated skirts, or jeans and hospital scrubs. She didn't explain when Margy admired it.

"Feel," Isa said, holding out the piece that looped over her shoulder. It was apricot silk, bordered in cream, and it glowed against her olive skin. "Isn't it delicious?"

They talked about David's new lab, and the progress of Webster's book *(Lake Death: Canary in the Mine)*. Isa described the grueling regime of her fellowship in cardiology, widening her big black eyes. Margy listened, smiled, and nodded. After the first few awkward moments, seeing David and Isa again, everything seemed to be fine. She didn't mind that they seldom spoke directly to her. She was used to Webster's friends. They were scientists, who dealt in facts, and she hardly knew any facts. She found it restful to be with them. She didn't have to air her opinion of a certain performance of the B-minor mass, or tell witty stories about the Kronos Quartet. She didn't even have to listen, all the time. And sooner or later someone would ask about her wrists. Decades of daily violin playing had toughened the fingertips of her left hand, made a sore spot underneath her chin, given her the carpal-tunnel syndrome in both wrists, and these were facts to interest Webster's friends.

She surfaced for a moment. David was telling Webster about a new machine for the analysis of protein chains. Isa pinched the sleeve of Margy's Italian sweater. "What's this? Pretty!" she said in mime. Everything was definitely fine.

They moved on to the Fourth Street Grill, for mesquite-seared salmon and shoestrings and chardonnay. Isa still drank mineral water. Finally Webster leaned forward, smiling.

"So, Isa. California appears to have gotten to you. Or is it cardiology?" He held up his glass. "Do you know something about this stuff we don't?"

Isa smiled, appeared to blush, and told a story about a by-pass patient who'd demanded wine with his hospital food, on the grounds that any meal could be his last.

"He'll probably live to be a hundred. I don't think there's very much wrong with wine." She straightened the fork in the middle of her plate. "Except at certain times."

She lifted her eyes at David. David nodded. He faced Webster and Margy.

"We have something to tell you, which is maybe a little surprising. We're with child."

On the wall above him, safety-orange chipotle peppers and puce eggplants danced in space.

Margy surged across the table. "You are? But that's *wonderful*. That's really *wonderful*."

The blood withdrew from Webster's skin, down his spine and into the chair. He couldn't look at Margy. The happiest moment of her life, she'd told him once, would be on the delivery table, when she saw her child.

David smiled apologetically. "It took us years to decide to do it. In fact, when we had our first pregnancy *scare*, we almost jumped out the window. But now that it's for real, it's strange. We're completely glad."

"But we had no idea," Margy cried. "Is that why you're wearing a sari? For maternity clothes?"

Grinning, Isa tugged the sari a little this way, a little that.

"That's what they're for. Infinite adjustability, no matter how big you get. You don't create a country of a billion people with a taste for tight clothes on women."

Briskly, cheerful as Mozart, Margy asked questions. She wanted Isa to know that it was fine to talk, that she was not upset that Isa was having a baby, while she was not. How did she feel? When was she due? What were her plans?

Webster looked mournfully at David. They'd never talked much, not about their lives. But they could take long runs on Sunday mornings, and sit together sweating when they got back, eating M&M's by the two-pound bag. David knew what to say at important times. When Webster was first married, he kept showing up at David's too tired to run, from making love to Margy all night long. "What do you think we're working out for, man?" David had said and grinned.

Webster tried to move his lips. Did David and Isa lie in bed in the mornings, reading and making love? Did they realize they'd never do that again?

"Do you realize," he said, "that the highest quality of life the human race will ever achieve is right now, in our lifetime? In places like this, where you can still breathe the air, and this class, which can still afford to buy a house? After us, it will be all decline."

David's eyes went slightly crossed. "Geez, is that true? That's a hell of a thing. So why can't you get a decent yo-yo anymore?"

Isa leaned forward with merry eyes, touched Webster's arm. Isa was from New Delhi, and she'd once said she thought America could use a little more population. "What about you two? Eh? Shall we expect an announcement?"

Webster smiled, a fissure in rock. Margy looked at him. So he hadn't told them, as she'd thought. Did he like the way this felt? Did he realize it was his fault for not telling them?

Isa touched her arm, wheedling. "I know that coy look. Hmmmm? You're already trying, aren't you? Temperature in the morning, dots on a chart?"

Beside her, Webster shuddered, like a glass about to shatter from a high-pitched sound. Margy lifted her chin.

"We've decided not to."

Isa's hands drifted down to the table. "You've what? But you can't do that. How could you decide a thing like that?"

Her eyes protruded at Margy, bright examining lights coming on inside. Margy uncrossed her arms from in front of her chest and made her hands relax at her sides. You never knew what Isa was noticing. She'd noticed some odd things herself. Since coming back to Webster, she'd noticed she didn't like to sit or walk or even lie in bed without an arm crossed on her chest, gripping the elbow on the other side. When she tried to do without it, the front of her body felt amorphous, as if it were ballooning out, swelling and swirling like a soggy cloud, and only a steady arm could keep it in.

Isa waved her hand. "You'll change your mind. What are you worried about, your career?"

Margy could not explain. It wasn't her career. She had a low chair in one of the world's best orchestras, and if she never got any farther than that, it would be fine. It wasn't even exactly Webster anymore. Lately he had said he didn't want to do it, no, and it would ruin what they had together now, which was awfully good, and since the earth was already buried in plastic diapers, it would be selfish to produce another child, but she could do it if she really wanted to, and now she wasn't sure she really did. Leaving Webster, she had learned an awful fact, that he was the one she wanted, and now she needed to lie with her head on his chest, while he soothed her like a baby. If they had a baby, Webster would hold the real baby instead, and when she wanted to put her head there he might say, "Pardon me, but you see I've got this real baby here. And would you mind cleaning the bathroom?"

He felt for her hand, and it was hot and dry, as if she had a fever. He gave her a glance that meant she didn't have to answer, but she didn't look at him. She tossed back her hair.

"Webster doesn't want to," she said. "And the choice does not mean much, does it, if the answer always has to be yes?"

Isa pressed her lips together, black eyes bulging wide. David tipped his head back, gazing at Webster as if he were a little too far off to see. He was not, Webster noticed, wearing a tie.

〜

They drove up the hill toward Walnut Square, planning to end with coffee-chocolate mousse and Meyer-lemon tart at the Chez Panisse Café. The evening had grown chill as cold white fog slid in, falling over the last mauve light like a lid. In Walnut Square, they had to park several blocks from Chez Panisse. Walking, they continued to talk, sometimes a little self-consciously, a little artificially, as they broke down to single file or stepped out into the street to avoid a homeless person, while pretending not to notice they were being asked for money.

"Of course," Margy said, stepping off the curb in her high heels, avoiding a suntanned man in a dirty quilt, "you won't even have to have amnio, will you? You're so young." Margy was thirty-five, and Isa at most was thirty-one.

"Spare change?" said the man.

Isa strode along with a relaxed expression, one end of the sari floating behind her like a wing. "Oh, no. I'm going to have it. It's always a good idea with geriatric pregnancy."

Webster stepped around the suntanned man, avoiding his eyes, and David followed him. Ever since Margy'd told them, David had stayed near him, shoulder almost touching his, not saying anything but letting Webster know he understood. Webster walked beside him in grateful silence.

"Geriatric?" Margy said. The edge of the sari almost brushed a car, but she caught it as she stepped back onto the sidewalk. "Who are you trying to kid?"

Isa laughed and looked at her. "I'm old enough to be a grandmother in some parts of the world."

A big black man with red eyes blocked their path. "I'm homeless and I'm hungry and it's my own fault. If you could lay a five on me—no, okay, then God bless."

They parted to stream around him and re-formed. A few steps farther on, a blond man in a button-down shirt held up a sign, "Disabled Vet." When they didn't stop, he shook it frantically, grimacing and weeping. In a doorway, on a pile of bedding, a gray-haired Chinese couple sat with their backs to the sidewalk, the man exhaling acrid smoke, the woman cradling an ornate platter on her lap.

Margy fell back, depressed. She couldn't give them money without making a scene, because Webster carried all the cash when they went out. He liked to know how much they'd spent, and she didn't like to lug a purse. He was yards ahead of her now with David and Isa, and if she wanted even a quarter she'd have to interrupt.

Isa turned, called gaily back, "Besides, I want to know everything. I want a laparoscope, full time, so I can watch the whole thing. But all I have so far is the sonogram. All I know is that it looks like a salamander."

David hooked his arm around her neck and raised his eyebrows over her head. "Oh, yes, exactly like a salamander. There was this gray blob, see, and this black blob, and the gray blob wiggled a couple of times. Sounds like a salamander to you, doesn't it?"

Isa slugged him on the shoulder with her fist.

Webster waited for Margy, but she didn't seem to see him as she passed. Her face had an expression he'd seen before, a damaged look. I have been denied, it said. Clenching his teeth, he followed behind her. What did he care if she ignored him? Why in hell should he mind?

He should never have let it happen to him, marriage. It was like all those other awful relations, brothers and sisters, parents and children, the way it wired your tender parts to someone else's whim. He had enough electrodes on his balls before he met her, thank you very much. Why would anyone volunteer for any more?

A young man stood on the curb ahead, with a rip in the seat of his pants exposing a buttock to the air, the skin chapped raw and red. The four of them passed him in silence. Margy stopped, touched Webster's arm, let David and Isa get ahead.

He stared at her coldly. "What?"

She held her palm out, whispering, "Give me some money."

He touched his pocket. The wallet was in front, where the pockets were deeper, and he could feel it riding on his thigh. "What for?"

"Just give it to me," she said impatiently.

He'd heard that tone before. You are acting like a child, she used to say in fights. Grown men do not act like you. She'd left him for a guy who looked about fifty, pudgy, soft in the middle—but mature.

He started to walk toward David and Isa, who turned to watch. Hooking his elbow like an anchor, Margy tried to slide her hand into his pocket. He caught her wrist, kept his voice down.

"Not now, Margy." Releasing her, he walked ahead.

She was aware of many things. That she should let it go, that she'd be sorry if she didn't stop, and that she would stop if she had not been drinking wine. But she seemed to be propelled by something large and fierce, reaching through her like a puppeteer. Catching up to Webster, she restrained his wrist, and plunged her hand into his front pocket.

He did not resist. Lifting his arms away from his body, he made clear who was causing the trouble. She skipped a few steps up the block, worked the money out of the billfold, and tossed the wallet back. She walked away, head down.

He scooped the wallet off the sidewalk. She had taken all the cash. The pores of his face felt cold. He'd broken sweat. On his toes like a prairie dog, he watched her go. Was it going to be like last time, when she had patted his arm? *Don't worry, someone else will love you?* He felt the sweat slide down his chest.

David's big hand fell on his shoulder, gripped his trapezius. "Hey, pal. Everything all right? What's going on?"

~~

Their rickety metal chairs sat on the sidewalk, in front of a cavernous café across the street from Chez Panisse. David and Isa had steered him there, so they could watch for Margy. At the other tables, street people hunched in tattered sweaters, stocking caps and gloves with missing fingers, trying to warm their hands around glass mugs.

Isa shivered, rewound the top layer of her sari. David took off his tweed jacket and held it while she slid in her arms. She flattened the lapels over her neck and did not thank him. Sighing, she looked up and down the street.

"I thought you two were through with things like this?"

David gave her a warning look. She smoothed the jacket's cuffs.

"You'd think it would be enough for her, the way you took her back, after what she did."

"Isa," David said. He picked up his cup, held it in front of his mouth.

"That was more than some men would have done." She gave David a sideways stare. "I'd hate to see what would happen if I tried something like that."

David's elbows barely touched the table top.

She tugged at the sari under the jacket. "I really would. What would happen if I tried something like that?"

His face settled like slag. "Are you sure you want to talk about that?"

Webster looked away, trying not to listen. On the curb across the street, the man with the hole in his pants stood waiting for a light to change, though he was in the middle of the block. Up the sidewalk behind him, Margy strode, swinging her arms. She looked fresh and relaxed and innocent, as if she'd just gone off to milk the cows.

Snapping his fingers, the man whirled. He charged toward Margy, averting his eyes. His hair was matted like a bird's nest, and a shining stream flowed from his nose, clotting in his beard. Snapping his fingers again, he spun back to his spot on the curb.

Margy passed him slowly. She didn't have much money left. She'd given a five to the red-eyed man who asked for it, and a ten to the disabled vet. She tried to give a twenty to the Chinese couple, but the woman waved her hands and shook her head. She left a wad of ones on the bedroll, hoping the man would pick it up. Her last two ones she gave to the suntanned man, and a ten to an old black woman she hadn't seen before. All she had left now was the twenty.

The man on the curb continued to remember errands he'd forgotten in the opposite direction. Margy fingered the sleeve of her sweater. It was rose-gray silk, shot with shimmering threads, and all she had to tie around his waist.

She held out the twenty. He looked at Margy serenely and did not take the bill. Gingerly she reached for his wrist, turned up the palm, curled his fingers over it. Pointing at his bottom half, she waved her fingers up and down. He had a musty smell, like a wild animal.

"That's twenty dollars, for new pants. Don't lose it. Okay?"

He did not look at the money. When she walked away, he still stood with his hand raised to the level where she'd let it go.

She spotted Webster and the others across the street. They didn't wave, but she knew they could see her as she crossed. David and Webster sat close together, while Isa slumped, staring down into her cup.

Margy got a chair from one of the other tables. No one spoke for several moments.

"Well," said Isa, putting down her cup. "So, Margy. How're your wrists?"

～

Webster was driving, and too fast.

"Get in," he said, yanking open the passenger door, after David and Isa dropped them at their car. Margy leaned back, trying not to watch the road. The fog had vanished, and ahead the bridge was a necklace of cold white stars against black sky. Across the water, San Francisco shimmered, yellow lights molding over rolling hills, like a lolling female body in gold lamé. Bright streaks dangled away from it, undulating with the waves.

Webster leaned across her, jerked open the glove compartment, and threw maps out on the floor. Margy clutched the handle on the door. "What do you want? I'll look, you drive!"

"What do you think I want? The bridge is a buck!"

In the gritty felt of the glove compartment, she found a paper clip and a plastic pen. When she glanced up, they were flying past the turnoff for the bridge.

"Turn here!" she shrieked and grabbed the dash.

Swerving across three lanes, they raced into the toll plaza. "Carpool Free," said a sign on the far left. Webster aimed for it. "Carpool Is Three Persons," it also said, but the gate was up. He did not slow down.

"Webster! Stop!"

The attendant put his head out, pulled it back in fast. *Whoosh*, they passed the booth. A dozen lanes merged down to five, drivers jockeying for spots. Webster claimed a lane and blazed right through.

Her voice was high and thin. "Are you trying to get us arrested? Have you lost your mind?"

His voice was calm. "Let's not talk about losing one's mind. Let's not talk about throwing away eighty bucks on the street."

"Oh, it was not eighty."

"You don't have a clue about money, do you? You don't even know how much you gave away."

"Of course I do. It was . . . less than we spent on dinner. If you're going to be stingy, why don't we talk about that?"

She glanced at the road. He was about to hit an enormous Cadillac, banked with lights.

"Look out!" she screamed.

Webster wove around it with a grace he'd never noticed at lower speeds. What a relief it was to be driving. How had she ever cowed him into riding on the passenger side?

"You walk by homeless people every day," he said. "And I've hardly ever seen you give a dime."

"That's because you don't pay much attention to what I do. I do it all the time, when I've got money with me. When I'm *allowed* to have money with me. You're the one who walks right by them."

"So now you're going to get self-righteous. Do you really think you wanted to help those people? Or was the point to make a scene in front of David and Isa? There I was, trying to convince them I wasn't crazy for taking you back—"

"Oh, I see. You had to convince them of that. Thanks for telling me."

His eyes were on the road, hands on the wheel. He wasn't angry, only Margy was angry.

"Look, I realize you were in some kind of state tonight, from talking to Isa. Some kind of breeding frenzy. But I don't see why that had to make you—"

Leaping out of her seatbelt, she faced his profile, familiar as the blade of an axe.

"What an attractive phrase that is. Why don't you give a course in elegant speech for the home? Call it 'Thug Talk Made Easy.'"

They roared through the tunnel and out onto the second bridge, the lights of the city suddenly fat and bright. Webster kept his foot on the floor.

"Have you ever noticed how often you attack me, in how many different ways? I'm a thug, and childish, and stingy, and I've ruined your life. You seem to want to keep me feeling guilty, all the time."

"Oh, I do not. I never said—"

"Why is that? Is it to distract me, so I won't notice what you're doing? So the next time you call me up and say that you've been—"

"I do not!" She put her hands over her ears, knowing what was coming next. "I do not!"

"Opening your legs for a stranger—"

"You know it's your own fault that happened! You know it's your own fault I left!"

"My fault?" he said in wonder. "My fault?"

His brain felt suddenly clear and bright, starlike. He knew what she meant. "Webster doesn't want to," she could say any time she liked, and walk out with another man. Webster did not want to, and she did. That was her alibi. A thought shot through him in a blaze of light. Margy knew how to get what she wanted. Why hadn't she made it happen, if she wanted it so much?

He imagined a baby, a very small one, his. Of course he'd love the little salamander. He'd probably love it too much. He wouldn't let it out of his sight. The first time he'd found a real one in the wild, a California slender, tiny and black, he'd picked it up, stunned by its thread-sized fingers, tiny legs. How could anything so vulnerable stay alive? Leaving his hand, it climbed his arm, parting the hairs, and when it came to the bend of his elbow, it lifted its small, curved face to gaze at him as if he were the face of God. How could he let it go, in a world full of shoes and rakes and tires?

"The truth is, Margy, aren't you the one who doesn't really want kids? If you did, wouldn't you have made it happen by this time?"

She stared at him as if balanced on the head of a pin. Lifting her arm from the shoulder, she slapped his face, his shoulder, his arm, the side of his head. He caught one hand, but she hit him with the other. Striking his eye, she knocked out a contact lens.

The road ahead was now bright fuzz, sliced by the speeding blackness of her arms. Closing the eye without the lens, he just made out the road ahead, flattened into bleeding planes of light and shade. Reaching an exit, he spiraled down to a wharf and stopped.

She was no longer hitting him. Taking hold of her neck, he bent her back against the seat. Her face was a white blur, staring up an inch away. This was not real, it was a play, he could throw her out the window, drive the car into a post, put his fist through the windshield and grind glass into his wrists, but nothing in the real world would be changed. He jerked her throat to emphasize each word.

"If you ever hit me again, I will kill you. I will kill you."

~

Lying on the front seat, he searched his face. Only the tips of his fingers tapped spider steps. He checked his eyebrows, hair, neck, clothes, the plush upholstery of the seat, the steering wheel, the sandy floor. He did not find the contact lens.

One hand over the vacant eye, he faced the way she'd

gone, toward the rear of the car. To get the depth, he opened both eyes. On his left a row of round-topped warehouses humped along, running together and re-forming like nightmare elephants. On his right an elevated freeway sliced out of the dark, a giant wing aimed for his head.

"Margy?" She couldn't have gone far at this time of night. She didn't have a quarter to make a call. All she had was the Italian sweater on her back. "Margy?"

He walked for several blocks, calling her name. The water was close by, exhaling tide rot and diesel oil. Rotating his face like radar, he kept the smell on his left.

Suddenly he was in the dark, without a streetlight. He flipped around. The light had gotten behind him. She wouldn't be out there in the dark. The street along the wharf was wide, and cannily he crossed it to check the other side.

Ahead was an empty lot, a field with grass. Out in the middle, a figure crouched. He could see her hair, springing out around her head. He ran out into the field.

"Sweetheart?" She wasn't going to make him search till he got lost.

At the last second, she turned into a black plastic sack, stuffed with rags. He touched it with his foot. How could he have thought that was his wife? He darted back across the field the way he'd come.

He stopped. Brick buildings had sprung up around him. He turned in a circle, holding out his arms. Where was the wharf? What had happened to the water?

〜

The pier lay in a slot between warehouse walls, with a view straight up to the bridge. Out on the end, where breezes licked the frigid water, Margy crouched against a piling, knees to chest, sweater stretched down to her stockinged feet. As she was running out the pier, one heel had caught in a crack, and she had kicked off the other shoe. She couldn't see them in the dark. She could see streaks of greasy swells, in flitting greenish light, cigarette butts awash. One Styrofoam cup rode up and down on its side.

She pictured his face, yelling an inch away. Touching her throat, she tried to distinguish sore spots the size of fingertips. Once, making love on a summer night, he had left the prints of all four fingers and his thumb in blue bruises on her upper arm. She had to wear long sleeves for a week, and he kept taking off her blouse to see the marks. "Tiny, delicate creature," he had murmured, kissing them.

Distant sirens cried, broken by wind. The roar of traffic from the bridge began to subside. The dark was now as perfect as the bottom of a burrow, even the green light gone. With the piling at her back, the cocoon of sweater warmed. A wave of sleep passed over her.

How did people learn to sleep in public places? Resting her forehead on her knees, she closed her eyes, but couldn't sleep. Stretching out flat, she crossed her arms over her chest.

Yards below, water rose and fell with rhythmic sighs. Her hands and feet began to swell, until they felt like claws on an industrial crane, and filled with pleasure. She wanted them to keep on growing. Her fingers bulged up big as Florida. Uncrossing her arms, she let her belly go. It sprang up, huge and round, grazed the bottom of the bridge, ballooned in space. She was not a tiny, delicate creature now. She was a house, a city, a planet, home to rivers and oceans, forests and mountains, a food-delivery system, a sewer, a bed, all that was needed for sustaining life. If she got up and walked, she could dent the ground.

She imagined Webster where he must be now. In their hotel room, he'd wash his face, slide between clean sheets, stare at the dark. She'd open the door, trudge in, enormous belly first. Crossing to the bed, she'd shake the floor.

"Here it is. How do you like it?"

Webster's eyes would open wide, his face become polite.

"Don't hit me," he'd whisper.

And she would say, "All right."

～

Out of the darkness thrummed a huge white boat and searched the blank face of the water with its lights. Stark glare deflated Margy, pinned her to the planks. The pier had corners, cleats, a coil of thigh-sized rope and heap of rusty rags, etched with shadows in the light. It wasn't close, dark, safe, but airy space, part of the street.

The dark was blinding when the boat had gone. Springing to her feet, she felt her way along the rail. One shoe stuck quivering by its heel, the other near it on its side. She ran to the lighted street before she shoved them on. It was hard to run in heels, but a woman alone on a wharf near dawn had better not walk.

Ahead she could see an elevated freeway, then city streets. The wharf was empty now of cars, except one, a new American compact half in the street on the wrong side. Swerving wide, she ran beyond it before she realized she'd seen that car before.

"Kill you," he had said in it. "I will kill you."

She ran another block, cast back a glance. The car didn't only look empty. It looked derelict, left to drift.

Warily, she circled back. The doors were unlocked, and the keys dangled in their ignition slot, glinted in the faintly orange light. In the tray between the bucket seats lay the square gold key to their hotel, the only one they had. Turning away, she looked around. Where exactly had he gone?

She was alone now, in a way she had not been before, when she could aim what she was doing in his direction. Street breath passed over her. Nothing moved, but everything looked like it might the second she turned her head. Leaping into the car, she locked the doors.

She felt watched. Starting the car, she left the wharf like a hand off hot metal. Racing to the hotel, she did not stop for lights. Webster wasn't in their room. He'd left no message.

She called the police, and they asked questions.

"Has your husband been feeling despondent?" the officer said, and told her to call back if he didn't turn up in a few hours. She called David and Isa, woke them up. No, they had not heard from Webster, why should they? Was something wrong?

"Yes, no, I'll let you know. Sorry I woke you."

"Margy?" David said as she hung up.

She changed into jeans and sneakers, got back into the car. The dark began to fray as gray light leached in. It gave the empty streets an illusion of safety, like a person sitting next to her, doing what she did. Doors locked, windows shut, she rolled along the wharf and nearby streets. He was not in the all-night restaurant on Market. He was not asleep on the sidewalk in a doorway.

Passing the ferry building for the third time, she noticed a pedestrian tunnel to the landing. Through the tunnel, she could see a body lying on the ground. Parking the car, she checked the street and ran for it.

The tunnel stank of wine and urine. On the other side, a plaza opened over the water, with huge cement planters circled by redwood benches. On the benches, under them, mashing down the tall blue lilies in the planters, people slept. The preferred position was on one side, knees drawn slightly up, arms crossed over the chest. Most were prepared for cold, with a jacket or a blanket, a hat or a scarf around the head. But one had only a linen jacket, a silk tie. Lying on his side, hands between his knees, he'd flipped the sage-green tie over the side of his head, like a dog with one ear inside out.

She took a step closer. His lids snapped open. A spark lit his eyes and died as iron came down behind them. Neither of them moved.

Finally Margy took a chance. She raised her eyebrows, faintly pulled up the corners of her mouth. Bravely she held onto it.

He glanced away from her, closing one eye. She was mistaken if she thought they were all the way to smiling yet. It might be days or weeks before they got to that, if they ever did. But slowly, inch by inch, his frozen body started rising from the bench.

Harbor

~~~~~~~~~~~~~~~~

Margy woke to the feel of Webster's skin under her cheek. His big heart shuddered, and his sleeping breath rushed with a sigh, like waves. It was still a shock, the pleasure of touching any part of him, his back against hers as she slept, the pressure of his hip as they sat on a couch. It had been months since their almost-divorce, when they had called the lawyers, called it off. For a while they had gone on being furious, and shouted on the street in the middle of the night. They shouted in the kitchen and in bed, and then they went ahead and made furious, ecstatic love and shrieked like factory whistles as they came. Webster sometimes even shouted in his sleep.

But one afternoon, they had stood naked on a bedroom hardwood floor, in thin winter sun, to put wedding rings back on each other's hands. Soon after that, with no warning, the anger seemed to lift. It made them almost giddy. It made no sense, or maybe all the sense there was. Now as she woke, she asked herself: Was she angry? Not in the least. She was giddy with relief. Webster felt delicious next to her. When she was pressed to him, there seemed to be a fountain bubbling into her, elixir, manna, sustenance. Fitting herself around him close as she could get, she slept again.

His kiss woke her, the clean smell of his shaving soap. Dressed in a pink shirt and faded jeans, new wire-rimmed spectacles, he looked cute as a toy. She chuckled, half asleep.

"Laughing in your sleep?" he murmured in her ear. "You lunatic. I'm just off to lab. You sleep. I love you."

The happiness was still there when she woke two hours later and sat up on the hard futon. It was a beautiful fall morning, warm and clear. Sun glanced off yellow maple leaves outside their new windows. The room was almost bare, oak floor, old mantelpiece, grapes carved in the high moldings. After the near divorce, they'd realized they had to leave their Lincoln Park apartment, start again, in a new place. Besides, Webster in a rage had gotten rid of all their furniture and kitchenware and Margy's clothes. So they were free, with hardly anything to move.

They'd found an old rowhouse on the Southside of the city, in Hyde Park. The first time they saw it, the walls were purple, used syringes stashed under a loose floorboard, a century of paint obscuring woodwork and details. Broke as they were, they had been lucky to find anything they could afford, and had to do the work themselves. They sanded, painted, and refinished, made it theirs. They ate picnics on the porch, and made love on the floor in the upstairs hall, since it was the only space without a window and there were no curtains yet. In this house they used no birth control. Nature could take its course if it was going to.

Stretching, she stood and walked through empty rooms, high-ceilinged, airy, filled with morning sun. Webster's soft pj bottoms hung on the bathroom door, and she stopped to sniff his warm and yeasty smell. The room beyond the bathroom opened on both ends, a wide place in the hall, and they had started painting it with pictures on the molding that a child might like. Jellyfish and frogs and plankton, violins and music notes.

Going down the old back stairs into the empty kitchen, she made coffee. Webster had built a simple table, legs fitted into the top without a nail or screw. It leaned slightly, but pushed against a wall it could hold plates and mugs, and they had bought two lovely old hard chairs at a yard sale. Sun shone across the clean expanse of empty countertops.

Far off, in the empty living room, the phone began to ring, but she did not move. It rang and rang, with no machine to pick it up. It would be a wrong number. They had a new phone number here, and when they called each other, they signaled by ringing once, hanging up. They had to hide out for a while, the two of them, get used to their new life.

Washing her yard-sale mug, she set it upside down by Webster's on the counter, more pleased than if it had been old Limoges. She went up the bare front staircase (handmade, with a subtle curve) to bathe in the clawfoot tub. The bathroom was the only room that seemed furnished, white towels and washcloths, cheap and new. Louvers on the bottom of the window let in clear blue sky above. Sun shone in the water, rippling and wavering across a wall beside the tub. Filling it deep, she floated, not thinking at all. With just her nose exposed, she sank as she exhaled, bobbed up as she breathed in.

The phone rang again. No, it was a different sound, a loud preemptive zap, meant to penetrate the house. It must be the doorbell, which no one had rung before. Lifting her head, she listened, careful not to splash. Of course Webster had a key, and no one else mattered. Letting her head slide back into the water, she floated in the peace and beauty once again.

But the violin was waiting, and she had to practice before rehearsal in the afternoon. They were doing Brahms, a slushy symphony she hated. But she'd have to try to sound convincing anyway.

Letting the water out, she dried and dressed in shorts and one of Webster's outgrown hockey tanks, shrunk now almost small enough to fit her, close enough to practice in. It was liberating, really, to have none of her old clothes or things. Everyone should blow up their encumbrances, their miserable marriages, and start again.

Humming, she set the music stand up in the bare expanse of living room. Two mantels faced each other across gleaming floor, and morning sun streamed in the windows to the east. Soon it would reach the sunroom at the front, five windows wrapped around it, through which she could see yellow leaves, red brick on the house across the street. Taking the violin out of its case, she began to tune.

WRAAAA, the doorbell zapped, outraged. *WRAAAAAA*.

Stunned, she held her breath. Perhaps if she stayed motionless?

A young blond woman's face appeared in the first window of the sunroom, peering in. Margy recognized her instantly.

Tiffany was exactly who they had been hiding from, along with James and most of their old friends. Tiffany had bombarded them with letters, phone calls, and suicide threats, and Margy had already listened to her for several hours on the phone. When Tiffany was six, her father had handed her a baby duck at Easter time, on his way out of town for good. After the duck grew up, her mother had driven Tiffany and the duck out to a pond to let it go, and a fox had killed it in front of her. All her lovers had left Tiffany the way her father did, but Webster was the worst.

"Stubbed me out like a cigarette," was what she had said.

Nevertheless, she was a gorgeous (if bleached) blond, taller and younger than Margy by a great deal, and Webster said she had done everything there was to get the perfect body, liposuction, silicone, fingers down the throat. She also studied lake biology, Webster's own field. Peering in the window as if she had a right, she examined everything with cool blue eyes. But when she noticed Margy staring back, at least she had the grace to look startled.

"Tiffany!" cried Margy heartily.

Hearty cheer was how you talked to children, wasn't it? When they had gotten back together, the head of Webster's lab had asked him to make sure Tiffany got out of school in one piece, with at least a master's degree. Margy of course would have to help. She was a grown-up, happily married. She could handle this. She flung the front door wide.

"Come in. Webster isn't here. Would you like some tea, or milk, or something?"

Tiffany slumped in, wary and morose.

"I know. He's at the lab. I came to talk to you. Coffee would be nice." A smile flickered on her lipsticked lips as she gazed around the living room.

"We threw out all of your stuff," she said and strode toward the kitchen, as if she knew exactly where it was.

Well, not *threw out*, thought Margy, certainly. What was she supposed to say, *I know my chicken?* She smiled. Webster never threw out even a used razor blade. Some of her ripped-up clothes were in the car right now, and in his lab, converted into rags. Their furniture he'd given to benefit a camp for Native American kids where Margy sometimes taught the violin. Even at the time, that had seemed a clear enough message to counteract the rage.

"Yes, it's a wee bit empty, isn't it? The kitchen has two chairs, though. Come on in," she said unnecessarily, since Tiffany was already inside the room.

Making more coffee, Margy found cookies (only somewhat stale) and put them on a plate. While she moved around the kitchen, she felt the girl's eyes on her, studying her bony, aging, freckled legs and arms, her flat chest, frizzy hair. When Margy turned to her, she looked stunned, eyes propped open in astonishment.

She set down the mugs. "Careful of the table. It wobbles. Webster made it, and of course he had to do it without even screws or anything. The Miwok way, you know."

Tiffany stared at her blankly. Hadn't Webster even talked to her about his Indian obsessions? Perhaps there wasn't time. They'd spent only a few weeks in each other's company, and Webster had made clear that most of that had been in bed. Margy felt a warm flare in her cheeks. She gave one quick glance at the girl's expensive body. But Tiffany had put on flowing Katherine Hepburn pants, a loose jacket. What to wear to see your lover's wife? Margy almost liked her for having taken so much care.

Tiffany also appeared to blush under her poreless, porcelain makeup.

"It's him I came to talk about. I'm just hoping you can explain it to me."

"Well, I'll try, of course. What is it exactly you want explained?"

Tiffany looked daring, lifted one arched brow. "I know you have to think that it was not important, what happened between me and him. But it was, you see. He wanted to marry me. He *begged* me to marry him, about a week before you came back home. I can't even believe he ever looked at you again. It's not like him at all."

Margy shrugged good-naturedly. Marry Tiffany? Sure, there were those weeks in bed, and Margy had done something like it, more or less, with James.

"Marriage is a mystery," she said evenly. "I'm sorry you were hurt by ours. It was messy, bringing other people into it, and we certainly did. It was immature of us. But we were both hurt, you see, and using other people to try to hurt each other. Webster used you, I'm afraid. I hope you'll believe me when I say I'm sorry about that."

Vehemently, firmly, Tiffany shook her head. "No, you see, that's not the way it was. He may have kept this from you, but I think you should know the truth. I hate to have to tell you, but he was really totally in love with me. He said he was glad you left him, and it was really more like he left you. You see, he'd figured out you were this awful person, and I was wonderful, and he loved me. He—he told me things about you. Sexual things," she said and glanced at Margy boldly.

"Things he hated that you did in bed. They didn't sound real good."

"Oh, dear," said Margy with a quick, light laugh.

Sexual things? Well, surely nothing much. Okay, the last few months before she left, of course it all went wrong. But wasn't that to be expected, after all they'd said? She could recall one time, possibly their last attempt before she left. Webster had been shouting at her about something—driving the car too much, polluting the atmosphere?—and somehow they had started to make love. He had his head between her legs when Margy realized how furious she was. Putting the soles of her feet against his shoulders, she had shoved him out of bed. After that point, they were both insane.

"We were a little nuts then, I'm afraid. I hope no one was taping anything we said, because we didn't mean it half the time. We're trying to forget about it now."

"I know," Tiffany said patiently, as if she were the grown-up here. "But that looks like the weirdest thing of all. I have no idea why he's back with you. He never explained it. Did he explain it to you? Or tell you anything about me? He must have said something. It would really help to know what he told you about me."

It was like being with a golden retriever, Webster had said once, trying to reassure Margy. *Very cute, but I had to keep throwing the stick.* Margy grimaced. Did grown-ups always have to lie, smooth over things? She made her face sincere.

"He said you helped him at an important time, when he needed it. He speaks very highly of you."

It was true, most of it. Tiffany *had* helped him. It was much better that he had called her, and slept with her as often as he needed to, instead of using that kitchen knife while he knelt beside the bathtub drain. Tiffany had kept him alive for her. Margy tried to feel a tiny spurt of gratitude.

"Listen, someday you'll be married too. It's not like being with a guy for a few months. There's this deeper thing that can happen. It gets into your DNA. Sure, there can be bad periods in a long relationship. But if you're lucky, you'll find out you're connected in a way that you can't change. And that's where it begins, the happiness. You just have to give in and accept it, accept being happy. That's what we're doing now."

Tiffany also tried to make her face sincere. "I just want to make sure he's being good to you."

Margy tried to look relieved and grateful. "Well, that's happening."

But it seemed pathetic to say that now. How could she tell? It was too soon. What sexual things?

They were silent for a while. Tiffany widened her eyes. "Don't think I envy you."

"Of course not. Why should you envy me?"

Margy seemed to have trouble getting air into her lungs. She smiled at Tiffany, and felt herself turn blue. Tiffany swirled her cooling coffee in her mug, took a last sip, and stood.

"Well, thanks, I guess. Thanks for the coffee anyway. Guess I'll be seeing you."

"Sure, now that we live here near the lab. I guess you will."

Margy walked her to the door and waited while she walked out, closed it behind her. Neither of them said another word.

～

She spun around the house, up and down the stairs, splashed cold water on her face. She felt a sudden urge to sell the house and flee, how far? Someone would find them, anywhere they went. James sent his letters to the symphony, and he had called there, sent a short blast of telegram *(You ought to be ashamed of yourself)*. He also wrote to Webster, asked to meet with him, but Webster refused.

"What planet is this guy from?" he said. And he was right, clearly. When you exploded your life in pieces in the air, better not to listen to the people on whom they fell.

She had to practice fast and dress and drive uptown. She kept her mind on Brahms, trying to think *impressionistic*, not *slushy*. In the second movement, she needed to underplay, slip under the hearer's consciousness. When you want to be heard, whisper! she shouted to herself. Don't think so much when you play. *Sexual things*, her mind murmured. *He begged me to marry him.*

At Orchestra Hall, she avoided the locker room downstairs, where her friends would be, and slipped straight into her place near the back row, began to tune. As her friends came in, she pretended to be absorbed. Mirasu was one of them, a gray-haired Asian cellist with a bitter mouth. Her only husband had gone on to marry two more times, each wife a decade younger than the last. Mirasu had laughed when Margy said she was going back to Webster. Did Mirasu know something she did not, that it was never possible to trust at all?

One day, making love to Webster, she had noticed she was flopping underneath him like a salmon out of water, helpless, holding nothing back. She felt afraid. Didn't men use sex to make you helpless, so they could laugh and walk away?

Then she had noticed he was also thrashing the same way. He seemed a trifle helpless too. Since then, she almost trusted him. She might as well have given up her skin, been flayed. Was it even possible she could survive if they broke up again?

Exhausted, limp, she tried to think about the Brahms. It seemed like endless hours that she had to play and play, barely holding on.

There was no concert that night, thank God, and she could get into the car and inch through traffic, lumber home. When she let herself into the house, the autumn evening light shone gold across the empty hardwood floors, stabbing her with beauty and betrayal now.

"Mouse!" called Webster happily, from the kitchen in the back.

When she went in, he was rolling pasta dough with just a rolling pin, since he had thrown out their machine. He stood expectant with a dishtowel on his shoulder, face a study in de-light. He had two wine glasses on the table, and a bottle of good red open on the counter. Leaning over, he kissed her six or seven times.

"Okay day?"

"Fine. Mostly fine."

"What's mostly?"

She examined the vegetables he had put out, started washing the asparagus.

"Your lab seems to give out this address."

"I don't think they do, actually. Why do you say that?"

She found a knife, roughed up one spear. "Oh, nothing much. Just, Tiffany dropped by for coffee."

"Ouch."

He smacked his forehead, left a flour print. "She could have followed me, I guess. How did it go?"

He held his hands out fast.

"*Not* that I want to know. I'm afraid I can imagine it."

"Did you tell her you planned to marry her?"

He let his air out in a rush. "I don't think so. But anything is possible."

"Do you like the way I make love?"

"Ha!" he laughed, one unconvincing burst. Grimacing, he sobered, took the knife out of her hand.

"Let's not discuss this with one of us holding a knife, all right? I'm extremely sorry that happened today. I'm sure you realize she came here to hurt you. She's not as helpless as she looks. I guess she managed it."

Gingerly, he wrapped his arms around Margy and sighed.

"What do you think, that I do this to torture myself? Let me tell you something. You are the sexiest woman I've ever known, and the best lover. I've never been bored with you for one second. You're the one who walked out on me, remember? I had to crawl through flames to get back to you. I'll crawl through flames again if I have to."

"And you don't wish that you had married her instead and had a young wife with a perfect body who never did bad things to you?"

"No. I would have been the saddest husband in the world, and the most bored. I wouldn't even have known what was wrong with me, or how good life could be. Look, you have to believe me. You have to. Okay, now I'm too anxious to eat. I need some reassurance here. Let's forget dinner and go upstairs."

Who should you believe, your husband, or your ex-girl-friend-in-law? Which one will make you happier? There was the truth, and then there was the feel of his body. The pasta could dry out and crack. The wine could turn to vinegar. Drying her hands on his paint-splattered jeans, she leaned against him as they turned to climb the stairs.

Canary in the Mine

~~~~~~~~~

She was not supposed to laugh, or cry, or think of anything. She was supposed to lie still on her back, while needles dripped a drug into her arm. She was pregnant, but she wasn't good at it. The first time the doctor had told her the good news, it lasted about a week. Then she got in bed with her own husband, and a pool of blood began to spread across the sheet. The second time, she had just left the office of her obstetrician, who had said everything was fine.

It might have been for the same reason it had happened to her mother, whatever that was, or because of drugs her mother took to have Margy. Or it might have been the British doctor with his horrible long knives. Whatever it was, her doctors now made clear that this would be her final chance. She had to give up her whole life, as if this really were her only purpose now.

They wired her to electrodes, needles, IV drip. Beta-blockers stopped contractions of smooth muscle, and could also stop her heart. After ten weeks of lying on her back, could she remember how to play the violin? For that matter, she wasn't sure she could walk. Astronauts' legs, they said she'd have, valves in her veins relaxed, blood changed from a river to a pool. All the hours she had spent trying to tighten her vibrato, round her tone, years of work to make it all sound effortless. Now she was just a lump of failed biology, here on the bed.

"Hey, you. You in there," she said.

Rat-a-tat-tat, the baby's heartbeat boomed out of a monitor in polka time. Her belly rose up like a speed bump, pale blue in the flannel gown.

Lightly she tapped against her drum-tight skin, beating out the "Blue Danube Waltz." It was all she could think of, and it was maybe age appropriate, for the minus-three-months set. The baby was just palm-sized now, but it could hear, and think, wonder about the tapping sound. Only, the trouble was, it couldn't breathe.

"Hey, you. You in there. Don't come out yet, you hear?" Tap-tap-ta-tap, she went. "Stay where you are, okay?"

Her windows looked out toward Lake Michigan, where it was February, gray water crossed with waves. Thin light filtered through the window to the gray linoleum, the metal bed frame like a paper clip, the rolling bed tray like a staple that fit over her. On the ceiling hung a water spot like a man in a chef's hat. It was her sole decor. She had been in too long for flowers, even cards. Her friends were sick of it.

"You're *still* in the hospital?" they said when she called. "Do you really think this is a good idea? Some people aren't cut out for parenthood, you know."

They sent her books, self-help psychology, as if pregnancy were something she should snap out of. Even her pregnant friend, Eileen, called only to brag about her "third-trimester bliss," how big she was, how huge her baby was going to be. What had ever made her think she liked Eileen?

"Nine pounds at least!" she crowed, while Margy thought in ounces, days. The start of the third trimester was a mirage that hovered, still a week away.

Suddenly the ceiling came down over her like shrink-wrap. The man in the chef's hat was now a quarter inch above her nose. She couldn't breathe. The hospital shrank tight around her, like a body bag. It happened several times a day, this strange contraction of the room, as if she were a baby in a womb, about to be expelled.

Groping with one hand, she found the phone, tapped in the

number of Webster's lab. Just talking to him sometimes made the ceiling back off from her face. But now his taped voice answered, gruff, inscrutable. He would be off staring at pond scum through a microscope, or intoning his prophecies of doom to undergraduates. Nature was nearly dead, he said, like his long-lost ancestors. Pond plankton was dwindling, and when it went, the rest of them were going too. Miscarriage was on the rise. After her first, he had sat at his computer weeping till he proved it for the city of Chicago, and St. Louis, and Detroit, and then for farms within a two-mile radius of some Midwestern ponds. Soon he'd have the model working on a global scale, and publish it so anyone could find the ratio of ghost shrimp larvae to fetal death in remote regions of Manchuria.

The door swung open, and the day nurse strode in, a large black woman who took in the situation at a glance. Nurse Jones had grandchildren, though she was only thirty-five. Margy was thirty-six, and she resented this. Nurse Jones assumed that Margy was an idiot, unable to manage even one live child, and wasting all this nursing effort in a bed where fifty capable young women could have punched out babies by this time. Standing by the bed, she turned back the coverlet.

"You have to stand up now, missy. Your claustrophobia will not improve unless you do."

"I'm not claustrophobic," Margy said.

Stand up! What were they thinking of? It could be over in an hour, the baby dead. She smiled sweetly.

"You should have seen me last night. I hiked half a mile up and down the hall. My husband helped. We trotted all around the ward."

The nurse flipped back her gown and peeled off the electrode from her belly skin.

"None of your stories, please. Let's go. I know you haven't been up on your feet."

Margy felt sincere, as if it were the truth.

"I'm just tired now, from all that walking yesterday. Maybe later on."

The nurse jabbed one finger in the air.

"I'm calling your doctor." She left the room.

Margy felt a squirt of glee. Wiggling around, she reached for the electrode, taped it back onto her belly skin. The monitor began to beep. She froze.

It was just a small contraction, ripple of faint pain. It might be from wiggling around, or from the glee. Any feeling could be too much now. In her fourth month, Webster had kissed her, cupped her breast. She ended up down on the labor floor. They had to raise the beta-blockers, barely made it stop. Her doctor said they couldn't raise them any more, it would be too much for her heart. Now she and Webster did not touch. She had stopped reading, watching TV. She tried not to daydream. Breathing deep, she closed her eyes and made her mind as blank and innocent as outer space.

The beeping stopped.

A thought floated by. It seemed harmless. Was it Wednesday? If it was, that would explain where Webster went. He would be up in Lincoln Park, with Calvin. Wednesdays were her day with him, and Webster took them now, drove him to doctors, pushed him out in his wheelchair. Calvin was coming back from Pneumocystis, holding off the megalovirus, skin marbled blue from Kaposi's. Picking up the phone, she tapped his number in.

"Hey, girl, you still in the missionary position?" his voice said, somehow still warm and deep. "I thought I warned you about that. Watch what you let boys do to you. You might get stuck."

She didn't mean to laugh, it just sneaked up on her. A light, happy laugh that left her lungs like a small flock of pale blue moths that had been trapped in there and itching to get out. A second passed, and she was fine. Two seconds passed.

And then the pain clamped down like monstrous teeth. She had no idea there was pain like that. She couldn't move. The monitor against the wall let out a high-pitched squeal.

"I can't talk now," she whispered.

Calvin laughed. "Hey, you called me, remember? Pardon me for interrupting you."

The phone fell from her hand. The call button was too far off to reach. The pain ground its jaws around.

The door swung open, and the nurse swept in. Eons later, when she returned, the gurney was behind her, clattering. A tall black orderly helped her to wrestle it through the door.

"Ready?" Nurse Jones said as she took hold of Margy's legs. The orderly slid arms under her back.

"Where are you taking me?" she gasped.

"The labor floor."

"No." She wrapped her hands around the metal bar along the bed. "It's too soon. It can't start yet."

"It's already started."

They heaved her to the gurney, and pain rushed out like boiling acid, filled the room. She made a sound she'd never heard before, like a panicked animal. Clipping her IV to the rail, they rolled her fast away, through hallways full of happy people, whose children were alive.

～

"Lake Michigan is a dangerous body of water," the sign said, half encased in ice, as Webster rolled the wheelchair out along a point in Lincoln Park. Icebergs on the beach loomed like dead whales, honeycombed and brown. Snow lay like Styrofoam on lifeless lawns. He had bundled Calvin up as best he could, in a down jacket, long johns, and wool pants. He was so thin the flesh showed through his skin, dull red, not like sunburn, more like he'd been flayed. Muscles stood out, sinews, bones, the whole anatomy. Calvin tipped his head back, trying to inhale around the clear tubes in his nose.

"Ah, nature," he said and pointed toward a grove of ratty pines. "Let's go over there."

Calvin had always claimed to be afraid of trees, saying they offered shelter to axe murderers and rattlesnakes. He preferred the comfort of nice asphalt alleyways.

"You sure?"

Calvin waved a bony hand. "What are they going to do, kill me?"

Webster rolled him into the grove and found a place out of the wind, in thin sun, where traffic roar was blocked from Lake Shore Drive. There was a good view of the shore. Calvin appeared satisfied.

"Driver, you may park the vehicle."

Webster set the brake and checked the dial on Calvin's oxygen. He never should have brought him out like this. But what was he supposed to say when Calvin asked for "one last picnic"? He was helpless now, with Calvin, with Margy. She lay fragile as an egg and never asked for anything. And the baby's heartbeat, with its hopeful thump. Under the skin of Calvin's balding head, blue veins pulsed visibly. Webster pulled his watch cap off, put it on Calvin's neck.

"Hey, I'm cooking in here," Calvin said mildly. "It isn't cold, you know. Feels more like spring."

"February 19? Not likely. There should be ice here six feet deep. It's more like global warming, killing everything."

But it was true, the air had a certain poisoned sweetness, as if factories nearby were turning out Twinkies. Unpacking their lunch, he handed Calvin a sandwich.

Calvin inspected it. "I like my tuna fish with little bits of dolphin in it."

"Don't worry. There should be at least a few endangered species there."

"Oh, good." His brow cleared. He began to munch contentedly.

Webster wasn't hungry. Taking a vial out of his pack, he

walked down to the water, plunged it in. The water felt suspiciously tepid. Capping the vial, he flipped open his pocketscope, squinted against the sky. Nothing in there, of course. Globs of old rubber in steel-mill effluent. Sometimes he found the larva of an armored worm, or of a plankton lamprey doomed to tumors as it grew. In May each year the lake still barfed up sick salmon to gasp in dammed-up inlets where their ancestors had spawned. Ah, nature.

"Hey, Mr. Science," Calvin called, rasping.

He walked back up the breakwater. Calvin's sandwich was only a little gnawed.

"Eat that," Webster said.

Calvin ignored him. "What are those over there? Big rats?" He pointed with his sandwich up the beach.

Webster pushed the glasses up his nose. Past some ice floes, he could make out two brown lumps. Fumbling for his pack, he pulled out field glasses and focused them. Beside a trash can stood two Canada geese, motionless as lawn ornaments. He handed the glasses to Calvin.

"Goose derelicts. Spent the winter here, on trash. They'll end up hanging by their feet in some Chinese restaurant. Might as well be rats."

Calvin peered into the field glasses, handed them back. "You take such a hard line on city life. Or is it all of culture you don't like? All the evil work of humankind?"

"Unreasonable, I know. It's only killing all of us."

Calvin stuck his thin chest out and tapped on it. "It's not killing me, bub. The *natural world* is killing me. Last time I looked, viruses were part of it."

"But not the airplanes that brought this particular one to you. In the natural state you never would have gotten it."

"Oh, I see, the natural state. How far back do we have to go? Me in a hut in Norway, you learning to skin buffalo? I'd be dead for sure of some childhood disease, or at least bored to death. Come on, admit you wouldn't want to live without Chinese restaurants. Just once, before I die. It's my last wish."

"How many last wishes are you getting? But all right. Maybe potstickers."

Calvin grinned. His lips were blue. Webster pointed at his sandwich.

"Eat that, would you? Next time we're going out for Peking goose, some nice warm restaurant. Besides, I have to call Margy."

Calvin made a face.

"Oh, don't worry, the Queen Bee is fine. I talked to her a while ago, and she was bossy as ever. A bit of attitude, in fact. I think all that room service is ruining her personality."

Webster waited while he ate, packed up the trash. Turning the chair across dead grass, he took the most direct route back. Calvin gripped the armrests as the chair bumped over frozen ground.

"Whoa, Nelly," he said, tipping his head back. He seemed to study the sky. "What is that? I hear a most peculiar sound."

Webster kept rolling. A quarter mile away, a thousand cars a minute thumped through potholes over Lake Shore Drive. Somewhere in the city, chemicals splashed on the ground. Another ton of hydrocarbons rose into the air.

"I don't hear anything."

"No, really. Stop a second. It sounds like a crowd roar. Bravo. Brava!"

Flourishing one hand, he gave a seated bow.

Webster stopped. He could hear something now, like voices muttering. Not voices exactly, more like bleats. It seemed to come out of the sky. Craning back his head, he looked, but could see nothing but some sooty veils of cloud.

"Must be a crowd somewhere. An angry mob. Demanding eight more lanes on Lake Shore Drive."

Suddenly he saw them. Necks stretched out, their wings beat frantically as if too small for their bodies. Brown geese, white cheek patches, long black necks. Five hundred in a V. No, more, a thousand geese, high up and flying fast. Behind them was another V as big. They flew north, up the lake, over a city of nine million people, five million cars, how many guns?

"Honk honk honk honk honk," they said, as if disputing how to go and where to land, and how soon would they eat? "Honk honk honk honk honk."

They flashed over, faster than he could have run. A minute later, they were gone. But another V appeared, and then two more, faint as smoke trails on the skyline, growing as they came, more lines behind, all down the twenty miles of city coast. Webster tried to add. Five Vs, five more, no end in sight. Some so high they almost disappeared, dark silhouettes against blue sky, a white half moon behind. A silver jet ballooned above the skyline, just up from O'Hare, and banked to miss the lines. How many geese across the sky at once? Ten thousand, twenty thousand, more?

"Honk honk honk honk honk honk honk."

Calvin shouted over them, "There's going to be some very lucky Chinese restaurant."

His face turned red, then white with cold. The sinking sun lit skyscrapers faint red. The lake shone with an emerald glow. Finally Webster rolled him home, legs almost too stiff to walk. But as they left, more geese flew over them, line after line in purple light.

~~

She smelled him first. He came in with the burnt smell of Chicago in his clothes, and hints of tuna, soap, formaldehyde. It made her gag. He held the rubber bucket while she heaved. She was just pain now, a machine clamped hard, and harder, crushing, crushed.

She tried to see him through the roar of it. He was the only color in this terrible new room, straight black hair, red shirt, flush of cold on his brown skin, red haggard eyes. Tears slid down the wide bones in his cheeks. They must have told him what she already knew. When the amniotic fluid broke, they tested it and confirmed that the baby's lungs were not developed yet enough to breathe. Not even with a respirator. If it was born now, it was going to die.

"We'll try to make it stop," her doctor said. They shot her full of drugs, more than she'd ever had. It didn't stop.

Webster pressed his face into the pillow by her head, clutching her hand. She tried to cheer him up.

"Love, honor, hold your puke bucket," she said.

Her mind felt strangely clear. She watched herself as if from far away, while pain crushed down, and all for nothing now. Too soon, too small, the baby dead, like all the lost babies. The two she'd lost, and the first one, in little pieces, eighteen years ago. Ann and Henry had had a baby boy, she'd heard, who had died in his crib. A violinist she knew had tried everything for years and finally conceived. But in the sixth month, they had said the baby's head was huge and full of water, and it would not live.

Margy wanted to make up for all of them. But she seemed to be a spaceship turning nose down to the ground, like the day they launched a woman science teacher into space, in a clear blue sky, schoolchildren watching everywhere. Margy had been visiting a Westside school that day, sent by the state to let the children meet a real musician, and she went to watch the launch with them. When the spaceship blew up in a puff of white, the children exclaimed with delight. Some of them cheered, because it was a teacher getting atomized.

"Take it out," a voice screamed through the wall. "Cut it out! I want it out of me!"

How far were you melted down when you called your baby *it* and begged someone to cut it out of you? Nature did not care about the individual, Webster had said. It wanted to start over with fresh combinations of genes, new possibilities, new cells. What the old ones suffered meant nothing. Her belly hunched up like a wasp stinging a caterpillar dead. The stinger jabbed in through her belly, tried to reach her heart.

"Take it out! Cut it out of me!"

Outside it was dark. Pale orange light shone from the streetlights to the windowsill. A minute took forever when you couldn't stand a second more of it. *Every Good Boy Does Fine*, sang some deep bank in her mind. *Bill Grogan's goat went up the hill. Kookaburra sits in the old gum tree. Sur la pont d'Avignon, l'on y dansa tout en rond.*

Someone wiped her face and pushed the hair out of her eyes. She'd never been so tired.

Suddenly, all was calm. She seemed to float above the bed, looking down. She could see Webster sleeping in a plastic chair, his head dropped back, mouth open, face creased like a seam. He had been sitting there forever, and she felt a rush of tenderness, certain she would never see him again.

Then she was on an empty stage, naked, alone. Webster walked on and told her calmly, being sorry, that he had stopped loving her.

"I don't love you anymore," he said. "Love is voluntary and sometimes stops."

She watched him jump off a tall building into a swimming pool, having a good time with his friends.

A roar of pain woke her. As she began to gasp, he jerked upright and took her hand.

She tried to tell the dream to him. He looked at her wildly.

"I'm going to love you forever. I already have loved you forever. Please don't die."

"Oh, I'm not going to die." Her voice floated dreamy in her ears.

Then the roar covered everything. Dials on the monitor swung to the highest number on the scale and just stayed there. The room was red.

He held a hand up to her mouth. "Bite me, please. Show me what it feels like. Please. Bite me."

What strange thing was he asking now? It seemed a small annoyance, far off, like a nagging sound. Dreamily, she bared her teeth and clamped them down into his hand.

～

Sometimes it's better not to be in your body. Crammed up in the top of her skull, she was trying to get out. She could not remember why they'd brought her here, into this awful brilliant place, silver metal gleaming all around, or what she was trying to do. It was too hard. Someone made sounds like a train out of control, metal-on-metal squeals.

The room was full of people in green gowns, white masks. For a moment, she could see her doctor, several nurses, the neonatal specialist. He was a man in his thirties who had already lost his hair, probably from all the infant deaths he had to see.

"Unnnnnnh!" she shrieked. "Unnnnnnnh!"

Two nurses held her naked, sweaty legs. She recognized the big hands on her arms, brown and capable, Webster's, one of them bruised. For a moment she could feel him all around her, holding up her back, his soggy shirt, his wet cheek, the shudder of his breath. Then everything went white. Her body started turning inside out.

"Don't push," a hard voice said. "Don't push. We have the head. Let it turn. Don't push."

She couldn't do it, but it didn't matter. She fell through space released, a puff of white. Now she was nothing and glad. This was where she had been headed all along.

Her body roared. She bobbed back into it and felt the weight. Opened her eyes, cold and sick.

A bloody mass lay on a green shroud over her. Masked people toweled and suctioned it. A baby's emaciated leg emerged, thin as a skinned rabbit's and red. It would have been a girl, with perfect feet and arms and hands, ten fingers and ten toes. The towels lifted to show a tiny hawklike nose, black hair, a face so thin the eyes bulged to the sides, translucent lids closed as if peacefully asleep.

"We have respiration," someone shouted.

Everyone stopped moving. There were little sniffing sounds. The baby's eyelids rose. Milky blue eyes glared. The neonatal specialist slid swift gloved hands under the tiny back.

"This baby is much better than advertised," he said and strode out of the room.

A rush of air like a big sigh lifted above the crowd of masked people.

"What does it mean?" cried Margy as she lay split open, on display as if filleted.

No one answered. The masked people bent over her, tugged something, made new pain. It didn't matter. Electrified, she plucked at Webster's flannel sleeve.

"Go with her. She's all right. I know it. Go with her, make sure."

The room seemed empty now without the baby. The baby was the most beautiful creature! "Did you see the way she opened up her eyes? Did you see that? Did you hear her breathe?"

Webster was crying, shivering, still clutching her arms.

"Go on, put me down. I'll be fine. Go see what's happening to her. She's going to be all right."

He lowered her a little but did not let go. He made an effort to stop crying.

"I don't want to leave you here."

"I know, but it's all right. Go on."

"We'll take care of her," a nurse said, and her eyes crinkled above the mask. She gestured with her head. "Intensive Care Nursery."

But Webster had already shoved the big door wide, onto the bright and empty corridor, trying to find his way.

Acknowledgments

The author wishes to thank the following magazines for encouraging her work by publishing earlier versions of many of these stories: *New England Review*, *Gettysburg Review*, *Threepenny Review*, *The Iowa Review*, and *Boulevard*.

And with thanks to Robert Hass, Wendy Weil, Jack Shoemaker, Jane Vandenburgh, Dawn Seferian, Trish Hoard, Connie Oehring, Linda Charnes, Joe DiPrisco, P. James, Irene Segal, Karen Heath, and the National Endowment of the Arts for their support.